"Freeze! Put your hands behind your head!"

Templar complied.

"Turn around, slowly."

Templar swiveled to face his adversary. It was the Russian named Ilya, armed with a Smith & Wesson 66. Ilya extended his empty hand. "The microchip, please."

Templar reached into his breast pocket, pulled out the precious item, and began toying with it. He rolled it between his fingers as a magician would a coin.

"Give it here!" Ilya barked.

As the words were spoken, Templar flipped the chip into the air toward Ilya. The thug's eyes searched in desperation, and his weapon wavered. In that split millisecond, Templar moved with the force of a compressed steel spring, kicking Ilya full in the head.

Ilya reeled from the impact, falling, his Smith & Wesson clattering to the floor. Templar chose that moment to flee.

He raced through the corridor toward the stairwell, setting off alarms and triggering a succession of unflattering photographs from a series of closed-circuit cameras. Ilya followed, cursing.

As for the Saint, there was nowhere to go but up. Fighting blustery winds on the rooftop, Templar sprinted to the balustrade. As he gripped the rail, a blast from Ilya's Smith & Wesson blew away a chunk from beneath his fingers.

"Give it up," ordered Ilya. "It's either that or fall ten floors."

"Easy choice," responded Templar, and he vaulted over the edge. . . .

THE SAINT™

A NOVEL BY BURL BARER STORY BY JONATHAN HENSLEIGH
SCREENPLAY BY JONATHAN HENSLEIGH AND WESLEY STRICK

POCKET BOOKS
New York London Toronto Sydney Tokyo Singapore

An *Original* Publication of POCKET BOOKS

POCKET BOOKS, a division of Simon & Schuster Inc.
1230 Avenue of the Americas, New York, NY 10020

TM & copyright © 1997 by Paramount Pictures
Cover art © 1997 by Paramount Pictures. All Rights Reserved.

ISBN: 0-671-00951-6

First Pocket Books printing April 1997

10 9 8 7 6 5 4 3 2 1

POCKET and colophon are registered trademarks of
Simon & Schuster Inc.

Printed in the U.S.A.

PART ONE

1

Hong Kong, 1970

THE ST. IGNATIUS HOME FOR FOUNDLING BOYS WAS once a warmhearted orphanage dedicated to improving the lives and saving the souls of Hong Kong's illegitimate offspring. By the seventh decade of the twentieth century, however, it had become as cold and unpleasant as its bleak, stony exterior.

Some one hundred boys, ranging from seven to twelve years of age, could call St. Ignatius "home." They didn't. They called it "The Prison," "God's Tomb," and most appropriate, "Brennan's Hell."

Father Brennan, a cruel and domineering discredit to the cross, lorded over the youths with harsh tones, severe punishments, and sadistic glee. His only kind words were reserved for his pack of high-strung Doberman pinscers—sinister, slavering creatures who shared his bed and personality.

Both dogs and boys jumped at the sound of Bren-

3

nan's voice, and all offered instant, exact, and complete obedience to the priest's shrill and insistent commands. All except one boy, the youngest and skinniest of Brennan's hapless charges. He was not intentionally rude and rebellious, he was merely mischievous and adventurous. Playful, outgoing, and possessed of a ready wit, his many talents derived from the unique pairing of his biological parents.

His mother was a versatile British actress best remembered for her lead role in the late sixties revival of Homer Quarterstone's famous play, *Love, the Redeemer*.

His Anglo-Asian father, a former bishop turned high-tech entrepreneur, created and implemented the Hong Kong production's dazzling special effects.

The couple's only offspring spent the first three years of his life immersed in a make-believe world where identities and locales changed with the application of makeup and the altering of backdrops. As with most theater families, they lived out of trunks and suitcases, called no man boss and nowhere home.

The child's world of endless make-believe ended in the famous Hong Kong Theatre Fire of 1967. Hundreds of patrons died that night, as did most of the cast and crew. The child, entrusted to a dedicated Catholic baby-sitter for the evening, was orphaned.

Devoid of kin, the thirty-six-month-old boy was shuffled from foster care to foster care before being secured permanent residence at the St. Ignatius Home for Foundling Boys.

His outgoing and entertaining nature earned him immediate friendships with not only the other lads, but with the young girls at the St. Patricia Home for Girls, the orphanage's female resident adjunct.

The likable scamp was blessed with limitless energy and a core of steely toughness that bolstered his resolve. Fueling his overactive imagination was the decidedly unorthodox reading matter he managed to sneak into the orphanage—tattered action-hero comic books, dog-eared paperbacks with lurid covers, and yellowed editions of *Thriller—The Paper of a Thousand Thrills!*

While the other boys studied Church history and memorized Bible passages, he delighted in blood-and-thunder adventures. The dreary reality of St. Ignatius happily evaporated as he escaped into a world of primitive chivalry, battle, murder, sudden death, damsels in distress, and valiant crusades for justice.

One particular and memorable morning, not dissimilar from any other in the seemingly endless chain of miserable mornings at St. Ignatius, the little rascal bravely smuggled his favorite paperback into Brennan's classroom, secured it behind his open Bible, and became completely absorbed in the action-packed adventure classic, *Knight Templar.*

He became so engrossed in the swashbuckling derring-do of its hell-for-leather hero that the numbing drone of Father Brennan's lecture never reached his ears. The high ceilings echoed back Brennan's boring discourse, but the avid young reader's mind and senses were far away from the cramped wooden desks and dusty stained-glass windows.

Wide eyed and grinning, he was knee-deep in adventure, neck-high in danger, and moments away from a real-life crisis.

The students were arranged in three rows of ten, with the St. Ignatius boys on one side of the room and the St. Patricia girls on the other. The youth sitting two rows over was called Bartolo. He would never have called himself Bartolo, but Brennan gave each charge a new name upon admittance to St. Ignatius.

"The answer, Bartolo," demanded Brennan, "what is the answer? What happened to Simon Magus in Sumeria?"

The boy hazarded a glance at the well-thumbed Bible on his scarred, wooden desk.

"Jesus' disciples performed miracles," began Bartolo haltingly, waiting for his fear to recede and his memory to surface. "When Simon Magus saw them, he offered Peter gold for God's powers."

Bartolo held his breath. Something resembling a smile distorted Brennan's face. The answer accepted, Bartolo cautiously exhaled.

Brennan's piggy eyes scanned the classroom, seeking another student upon whom to pounce. He found the perfect prey in a surprisingly happy youngster staring intently at an open Bible.

"And how did Peter respond . . ." Brennan looked directly at the reading child. "John Rossi?"

The boy behind the Bible did not respond.

"John Rossi." Brennan repeated the name slowly, ominously. The boy, immersed in an alliterative paragraph packed with adjectives and adverbs, ignored him.

Twenty-nine students cringed in their seats as Father Brennan crept up on the youngster and yanked away the Bible, revealing the gaudy cover of *Knight Templar*—a garish full-color rendering of mayhem featuring the semi-exposed bosom of a distraught female and an equally artistic representation of her manly hero.

Muffled giggles lost themselves in the rafters; perspiration dripped from Brennan's twisted upper lip. The boy threw a quick glance across the room to a darling, doe-eyed ten-year-old girl named Agnes. She enjoyed his antics, and her sweet giggle was music to his ears.

"What's *this?*" barked Father Brennan, grabbing the paperback and shaking it violently. The yellowed pages fluttered in the priest's grip like a sparrow captured in a falcon's talons.

Twenty-nine small hearts pounded in tiny chests. One heart remained calm—the one beating in the diminutive frame of the boy called John Rossi.

"It is," offered the lad helpfully, "quite an impressive adventure."

The response brought the desired reaction—the priest rocked back on his heels in affronted disbelief. Numerous small mouths gasped in astonishment.

"Adventure? How dare you speak of adventure! How dare you read this . . . this . . ." he sneered with disgust at Knight Templar and equal revulsion at the well-endowed jeopardized ingenue whose feminine charms seemed about to spill out over the binding, ". . . *trash!*"

Father Brennan angrily hurled the book across the room. It sailed in a flailing arc over Bartolo's head and smacked into the wall. The spine snapped and pages exploded in a flurry of falling pulp. Like a broken-winged bird, Knight Templar's greatest crusade lay lifeless on the ground.

Little Agnes jumped in her seat. Somewhere in the back of the room, a child began to cry. Brennan whirled and glared.

"Stop that this instant!"

He turned his attention back to the impertinent boy.

"Now that we have removed your distraction, perhaps you will recall that we were discussing Simon Magus of Sumeria," Brennan spit out each word as if an insult. "Now tell us, John Rossi, how did Peter respond to the magician Simon Magus?"

The youth looked Brennan directly in the eye.

"My name is not John Rossi, has never been John Rossi, and never will be John Rossi."

The child in back continued softly sobbing.

Brennan slammed his hands down on the boy's desk and hissed into his high-spirited charge's face.

"You and every other bastard lucky enough to be here . . . children of sin, spawn of the damned . . . are all named for *saints*—saints who were disciplined, saints who were chaste."

The boy's eyes were unflinching chips of iced lapis, never wavering from the priest's heated glare.

"You were named for John Baptist Rossi," spat Brennan, "a Capuchin priest who gave away his possessions . . . a man who had *nothing,* like *you!*"

The back row sobbing increased in volume. Brennan turned sharply and demanded silence. In that brief moment the boy who refused to be called John Rossi adroitly lifted a cruciform stickpin from the distracted priest's hem and quickly palmed it.

Brennan's attention was back on him in a heartbeat.

"Now, John Rossi who has nothing," sneered the triumphant headmaster, "what lesson have you learned today?"

The boy cast a casual glance at the scattered remnants of *Knight Templar.*

"Hardbound books are a wiser investment?"

The room erupted in gales of laughter, and Brennan exploded in anger.

"My cane!" yelled Brennan, grabbing the witty boy

by the scruff of his neck and pulling him from his seat. "Someone get my cane!"

Brennan scrunched his fingers harder into the boy's neck and shook him as he had done the paperback book.

The remaining youths sat frozen in fear as Brennan's red-rimmed eyes scorched across the rows of blanched faces.

"Bartolo," Brennan snapped impatiently, "fetch me my cane, *now!*"

Reluctant and torn, the boy squirmed and stared pleadingly at his classmate. The captive child managed an accepting glance, and Bartolo hastily did as he was told.

He scrambled from his seat, left the classroom, and hurried down the hall to the headmaster's private office.

Brennan's stiff bamboo rod rested on the bookcase behind a cluttered, heavy oak desk. Bartolo reached up and grabbed the cane, spun on his heels, and raced out of the office.

Panting and breathless, the unhappy errand boy delivered the stiff bamboo rod. Brennan snatched it and thrashed it several times in the air. Bartolo, trembling, returned to his seat.

"Perhaps, John Rossi, you would prefer being bastinadoed," growled the unrelenting headmaster, and the students gasped. They knew the pain and terror of the bastinado—tiny feet beaten bloody with stiff bamboo.

Even Brennan knew he could not bastinado the boy with any degree of justification, but a good caning was well within his rights.

The terrified child in the back of the room was now

wailing like a banshee. Agnes's face flushed, and tears rolled slowly down her cheeks.

"For God's sake, stop that childish crying!" yelled Brennan. "He's the one about to get a whipping, not you."

To escape the irritation of incessant sobbing, Father Brennan yanked his captive out into the corridor.

"Stand straight!"

The boy complied.

The class gathered to watch through a stained-glass window as Father Brennan swung back the cane and whipped the boy's backside. With each stinging slap of the cane, Brennan demanded the boy admit to the name John Rossi. Each demand was met by silence more confrontal than verbal rebellion.

No cry came from the boy because he was digging the stolen stickpin into the palm of his hand. The self-inflicted pain negated that administered by Father Brennan.

Twenty lashes later, with aching wrist and exhausted arm, the weary priest lowered the switch to his side.

"Really, Father Brennan," spoke the boy evenly, as if asking a pertinent theological question, "do you honestly believe I deserve such painful punishment?"

The priest instinctively raised the cane for another strike, paused, and seemed to give the question serious consideration before bringing the stinging switch down harder than ever. The child dug the pin in deeper, and warm blood seeped through his clenched fist.

"The name is Templar," whispered the boy defiantly to himself, "Simon Templar."

The headmaster, more frustrated than defeated, tossed the cane aside in anger.

"I'm not done with you yet," he snarled. "There

are other ways of convincing you. Go to your bed and don't come down until you hear the lunch bell!"

Experienced in the art of manipulation and humiliation, Brennan decided to utilize the most effective way of controlling a child's behavior—peer pressure.

That noon, when all hundred male residents of St. Ignatius were gathered in the dining hall for lunch, an empty plate was placed before each boy. John Rossi had, as instructed, joined the others at the sound of the bell. He sat next to Bartolo at a long wooden table.

The prepared food was displayed before them in an alcove cleared especially for the occasion, padlocked behind a wall of steel mesh.

Brennan stood between the first row of boys and the object of their desire.

"No meal will be served to any lad until *he*"—Brennan pointed to John Rossi—"acknowledges his namesake. Not one of you will be fed until he says his name, John Rossi, loud and clear."

Two hundred eyes turned to the skinny boy in hungry anticipation. The food at St. Ignatius was nothing to write home about, but these boys had no other home.

The youngster remained silent.

"C'mon. Just say it and get it over with," whispered Bartolo.

"I'll see him in hell first," the boy insisted pleasantly under his breath.

Despite the glare of his classmates and fellow prisoners, he remained mum. True to himself, he would not allow Brennan to define his identity; true to his word, Brennan left all plates empty at lunch and again at supper.

By lights-out that evening, ninety-nine boys harbored understandable resentment toward their smallest compatriot. Whatever admiration they felt for his bravery was outweighed by the hollow sensation in their bellies. If they could not eat, they could at least derive pleasure from pummeling the cause of their discomfort.

The skinny kid with the punctured palm reclined on his cot. He was thoughtfully examining the purloined stickpin. He was attaching it as an accessory to his crude, wood handled penknife when he noticed an ominous cluster of scowling classmates surrounding him. Before they could strike, John Rossi sat up brightly and spoke.

"Well, me hearty pirates, do you want supper or not?"

Surprised, they nodded.

"C'mon then!" He leaped from the cot as if on a mission from God. "Follow me to the free feast of the night!"

And follow him they did. They crept full of hunger and curiosity out of their sleeping quarters, descended the dark wooden stairs, and sneaked silently into the dining hall.

With hushed tones and soft steps, the boys approached the steel mesh. Behind it were loaves of bread and plates of biscuits, butter, and bowls of cold soup.

The wall of mesh was secured on one side by an old-fashioned padlock, which John Rossi gleefully attacked with the stolen stickpin. Working with intense concentration and near-psychic precision, it was only moments before his efforts released the lock.

The ravenous youths pushed aside the wire mesh

and helped themselves to a late-night meal, happily filling their stomachs and heaping admiration on their adventurous and courageous leader.

Forty-five minutes later most of the well-fed orphans were fast asleep when a single window on the top floor of St. Ignatius slid open high above the courtyard. Slowly, secretively, a long white snake of bedsheets slithered out into the cool night air. Behind the window, John Rossi and ten co-conspirators fed their thin escape route down the wall.

One by one they slid down, suppressing giggles of delight at their own bravery. John Rossi passed Father Brennan's open window on the way down. He paused, still smarting from the priest's whipping, and peeked inside. He could make out the huddled form of the snoring priest and the pack of slumbering Dobermans.

"Never again," whispered the boy softly as he continued his downward climb. "Never again."

With all his fellow escapees safely on the ground, John led the way to an identical building located catty-corner on the courtyard—St. Patricia's Home for Girls—which was also locked up for the night.

John began working the priest's stickpin into the front door lock. His pal, Bartolo, watched in admiration.

"They should name you Simon Magus, for the magician. . . ."

The little lockpick flaunted the heroic white cloak he'd fashioned from a sheet, with its red cross drawn in red marker on the left shoulder.

"Simon *Templar*," insisted John, "crusading Saint and—"

The lock popped open. Proud delight cut short his recitation. The young knights crept stealthily into St.

Patricia's, sneaking silently down the corridor. They flattened themselves against a dark wall when the exceptionally large Sister Teresa waddled down the opposite hall. As her flapping black habit disappeared around the corner, the ragtag crusaders continued on their quest. They climbed the stairs to the second floor, but on the landing their progress came to an abrupt halt—a heavy mesh partition, fit for a high-security prison, extended from wall to banister, floor to ceiling.

Bartolo looked eagerly at his leader but saw only an expression of disappointment.

"Someday I'll get in . . . *anywhere,*" insisted Rossi defiantly. He eyed the door to the girls' dormitory, a few short yards beyond the barricade.

He shook the mesh and called out "Agnes!"

The girl awoke with a start and a quick gasp, sat up, and glanced around. The room's tiny cruciform night-lights revealed several other girls were also awakened by this unexpected late-night visit.

Trailed by curious girlfriends and rubbing sleep from her eyes, Agnes left her tiny bed and walked barefoot out into the hall toward the landing.

"John Rossi?"

She saw him through the grim partition. Delighted and disbelieving, she ran straight to the mesh barrier.

Equally happy, he drew a golden strand of Agnes's hair through the mesh and began stroking it.

Although moved, she still managed to admonish him.

"You realize that when they catch you, they'll cane you."

Her hero would have no such doomsaying.

"It will never happen, dear Agnes, because tonight

this hearty brotherhood is leaving"—his eyes danced with lively mischief and joyous self-assurance—"on a Crusade!"

A delighted smile brightened Agnes's face. She not only believed him, she believed *in* him.

"Oh, John Rossi!" she exclaimed happily.

"I am no longer John Rossi," declared the boy with a triumphant wave of his cape. "My name is Templar, Simon Templar, crusading Saint and hero of a thousand adventures!"

He took her warm hand in his through the cold metal mesh. At that moment, he became the embodiment of all things altruistic and romantic. It was as if the fictionalized Knight Templar from the colorful paperback had come to life.

"I have risked everything, Agnes my love, to bid you farewell. I can't leave you without a kiss, can I?"

The boy was in his glory; Agnes's eyes misted in adoration.

"And where do you go? What will you do?"

The Saint errant tossed back his head, striking a piratical stance on the stairs.

"Why, we will go out and find more and more adventures! We will swagger and swashbuckle, and boast and sing and throw our weight around!"

Agnes giggled, her feet prancing on the landing.

"You don't weigh that much!"

The other children laughed aloud, forgetting the lateness of the hour and the danger of discovery.

Sister Teresa was returning from the bathroom when she heard children's happy voices—a rare occurrence at any hour. Worse, she heard *boys'* voices. The waddling nun ran fast, then faster, to the scene of the disaster. When she saw the unauthorized midnight conclave of underage children in their nightclothes, she screamed as if Satan himself had erupted from Hell.

Her high-pitched wail echoed through the courtyard like the screeching whine of incoming artillery. Father Brennan was awake in an instant, and so were his dogs.

Sister Teresa, arms flapping, turned in florid agitation, propelling her massive frame toward the main entrance in an overheated rush to summon Father Brennan from St. Ignatius.

Taking the sudden commotion as an exit cue, Simon Templar waved farewell with an exaggerated flourish. As the boys began their hasty departure, Agnes's voice sliced through the air.

"Wait! John Rossi. My kiss . . ."

He stopped, enchanted by the proposition. The other boys ran, but Rossi returned to the impenetrable barricade. There was only one way to do it—if the two heroic lovebirds leaned over the banister and around the partition, and if they both stretched, their lips would touch.

He, taller than she, leaned out over the twenty-foot drop, his lips at the ready.

She, substantially shorter, sweetly puckered in anticipation as her cold little toes left the floor. She balanced precariously on the banister, her lips brushing his, as the furious barking of dogs began echoing up from the stairwell.

When Brennan and his Dobermans arrived on the second-floor stairs, the unamused headmaster discovered the two in mid-kiss. A shaft of moonlight shimmered through the window, bathing the precious couple in serene, beatific illumination.

If hearts were touched by their innocence and appearance, Father Brennan's was not among them. A sadistic grin twisted his unpleasant features. The dogs snarled.

"Sic the boy!" the headmaster hissed.

Agnes's eyes opened wide in terror. The dogs leaped from behind John Rossi, barking and snapping viciously, and she involuntarily recoiled. Agnes' arms flailed desperately as she tried to regain her balance, but only her eyes caught Simon's before she disappeared over the banister.

Brennan called off the dogs and hastened to the edge. He and Templar stood side by side, looking down at the lifeless body of innocent Agnes crumpled on the cold marble floor.

Father Brennan turned in rage to the stunned and speechless boy.

"Bastard!" yelled Brennan, slapping the child across the face. "Who the hell do you think you are?" He slapped him again, and the boy's soul recoiled. Ice poured through his veins, and when he spoke his voice was steel on chilled steel.

"My name is Templar, Simon Templar." He tried to force the words out, but his faith had fallen with Agnes. A third slap silenced his youthful impertinence, and his once bright eyes became dark stones in a well of tears.

2

Moscow, Russia, Present Day

CNN CORRESPONDENT JAN SHARP'S NOSE HAD BEEN cold and numb for so long, she almost doubted its existence. Bundled against the freezing Moscow wind, she stood before the famliar backdrop of St. Basil's cathedral while her cameraman, Lloyd Swain, prepared for broadcast.

"This is what I get for majoring in Slavic languages and broadcast journalism," quipped Sharp. "I could have majored in Romance Languages and we'd be doing a lifestyle feature on the pleasure resorts of Spain."

Swain's laugh formed warm breath clouds around his large, gregarious face. He, too, was encased in thermal underwear, quilted parka, and heavy gloves.

"Been there; done that," replied Swain as he adjusted the camera's white balance. "Besides, if we don't cover this Tretiak story, Chet Rogers at UPN will get all the glory."

A sudden gust of iced wind compelled Sharp to tug her fur-rimmed hood tighter around her face. She shivered and looked over to her left for a quick glimpse of her primary competitor. Chet Rogers's UPN crew was also in Red Square, as were the folks from ITN and the big four American broadcast networks.

After a few more interminable minutes of wet, stinging air and last-minute technical adjustments, Swain was ready.

As the seasoned newscaster was about to begin, she noticed a long-haired tourist wearing a bright blue parka point his 35mm camera in her direction. She smiled her best professional smile, and he clicked the shutter moments before she went on the air.

"The Cold War may be over," intoned Sharp, "but the war against the cold is heating up with dangerous political implications. Ivan Tretiak, the ultra-Nationalist former Soviet minister of energy turned Moscow entrepreneur—the former National Oil Company is now Tretiak Industries—is about to give a highly publicized address projected here, in Red Square, on giant video screens. If he has his way, he will take control of the former Soviet Union, playing the current crisis into an opportunity for another Russian revolution."

The correspondent continued detailing the background of the crisis as thousands of Muscovites filled Red Square, huddling together in rapt anticipation.

"Moscow's National Oil Company building was, during the era of Stalinist Russia, the singular source of reliable physical warmth during a reign of icy terror. By the turn of the twentieth century, however, the demise of Soviet Communism and resultant rise of capitalistic entrepreneurism has brought another chill to the Russian people—a coal and oil shortage of numbing proportions."

The crowd stood shoulder to shoulder, cheering, stomping, and flicking their imported childproof lighters as an enthusiastic ovation for the dynamic leader who would soon address them from the heart of Tretiak Industries.

Giant video screens on either side of a double-headed eagle banner were filled with full-color images of Tretiak's October Party banner—a rising sun, and a Russian girl and boy gazing on a glorious tomorrow.

The image dissolved into the energetic, fortyish, and victorious-looking visage of Ivan Tretiak being broadcast from the dramatically lit conference room of Tretiak Industries.

He delivered his impassioned, articulate, and inflammatory speech as much to the cameras as to the cold crowd huddled in the streets.

"For eight centuries Moscow, our Moscow, has been the seat of true civilization," declared Tretiak, his voice echoing back from the cold stone buildings, "but now, what do I see? A Wild West town from some American movie!"

The crowd, familiar with American movies, cheered.

"If this is the Wild West, then make me your sheriff," he exclaimed. "Let me wear a star . . . a *red* star!"

Pandemonium. The crowd, predisposed to agree, chanted his name in wild affirmation.

The long-haired tourist in the bright blue parka squeezed his way through the crowd as Tretiak continued his diatribe against the current Kremlin leadership and the evil influences of American motion pictures. The bitter cold and equally bitter mob meant nothing to him. He casually exited Red Square, returned to his budget-priced hotel room, gathered his belongings, and secured cab transportation to the airport.

The man entering the taxi, however, did not have long hair, nor did he look American. The name on his passport did not match the name under which he rented the Moscow room, nor did it share any similarity to the appellative used upon entering Russia.

Neither the flight attendants in first class nor the well-endowed matron sitting across from him could ever imagine that this handsome and well-mannered young man had, only a few hours before, been pulling off one of the most daring robberies in Russian history.

Simon Templar had done exactly that, and accomplished it by thorough planning, precision timing, and unwavering confidence. Templar's confidence was well deserved. He had come to Moscow to do what he did best—steal. No longer a small, skinny lad, this handsome man had been self-reliant and self-supporting since his final escape from St. Ignatius at the age of thirteen.

The scene of the daring daylight robbery was the aforementioned Tretiak Industries building. Templar had acquired a small rented room not far from the target, and within days the walls were decorated with numerous telephoto images of the building from various angles, close-ups of specific individuals, and detailed floor plans.

A dedicated professional, Templar prepared for the caper with consummate skill. In addition to an astonishing collection of high-tech tools, he possessed total mastery of the art of disguise. His assortment of false mustaches, wigs, cheek pads, and mouth prosthetics rivaled the collection of any member of the Holly-wood makeup artists' union.

Simon Templar was, after all these years, still deter-mined to be the only one to define his identity—an identity he could change at will.

By the time he left his rented room for Tretiak In-dustries, he was a moon-faced, chunky, mustachioed ruffian enwrapped in a heavy quilted overcoat.

He was not the only ruffian in a quilted overcoat entering Tretiak Industries that afternoon. Several such men acted as bodyguard escorts for a cadre of tuxedoed Japanese and Russian businessmen at-tending a high-level business conference preceding one of Ivan Tretiak's polished media events.

Templar easily blended into the procession.

As they passed the formal security desk on the way to a bank of elevators, he quickly attached a tiny video camera, no bigger than a watch face, to a pillar di-rectly facing the security system's single video monitor.

Once inside the elevator, Templar hid his face by murmuring officiously into a walkie-talkie tucked deep in his shoulder. The others paid no attention to him, but one man seemed to project an air of suspicious unease. His name was Ilya, and it was his job to be suspicious and uneasy. In his hip Nike attire and Doc Martens, he was exported American excess personified.

No mere bodyguard, Ilya was the worst of Russia's new breed of immoral toughs providing personal secu-rity to Russia's capitalist elite. He was on Tretiak's personal payroll and under specific instructions that absolutely nothing was to mar this most important meeting.

The elevator reached its destination. The well-dressed occupants and their beefy bodyguards poured out into the hallway. Templar, staying inside the advance guards' blind spot, slid back to the service stairs.

As the entourage entered the conference room, everyone became swept up in welcomes, handshakes, and obligatory bows. Even Ilya initially failed to notice the bodyguard count was down by one.

Alone on the stairs Simon Templar removed his overcoat. The bulk underneath was not padding, but gear and paraphernalia which he transferred into a large backpack before beginning the climb to his final destination—the top floor of Tretiak Industries.

Meanwhile, one floor below, the businessmen gathered around a detailed scale model of a planned petroleum project. Champagne poured and toasts were made to the linkage of Japanese business to the New Russia.

Two of the more serious Japanese executives, politely wary, turned toward the window and surveyed the scene of potential turmoil in Red Square.

"The New Russia appears desperately unorganized," commented the shorter and more dour of the two.

"Who will keep order? Chaos does not bode well for business."

A sudden back slap caught both men's attention. Draping his arms over their shoulders was an outgoing Russian displaying a predatory grin—Yuri Vereshagin, chief operating officer of Tretiak Industries. He, too, looked at the clamor in Red Square.

"A time of tumult is also a time of opportunity for men of courage and vision," insisted the smiling Russian. "We have a word for it—*bespredel.* It means, 'no limits.' All of us at Tretiak Industries are dedicated to progress, guided by the all-embracing vision of Ivan Tretiak. Ah, if only he was in charge instead of President Karpov! Believe me, all around us are unlimited opportunities."

Several stories above them, Simon Templar's attempt to exploit opportunities of his own came to an abrupt halt. For security purposes, the final flight of service stairs was sealed off by a cement wall.

Undaunted, he backtracked to the previous landing and forced open the window. He reached into his backpack and extracted a foot-long sectional aluminum-alloy hook ladder which telescoped to twenty-five feet. In moments Templar was scaling the next two stories, clinging to the ultralight rungs in the pitiless winter wind.

By the time the two Japanese executives had been drawn into the formal proceedings, the efficient burglar had reached the rooftop. The only remaining obstacle was a standard door and a simple lock.

He chuckled softly to himself as he pulled a sleek penknife from his bootheel and began picking the lock. In an instant the door opened, and he stood at the entrance of an empty, undefended corridor.

From his bag of techno-toys came a pair of infrared goggles. Once in place, they allowed him to see the wall of horizontal light beams shining from floor to ceiling.

Under normal circumstances, any attempt to bypass these heat-sensing beams would be futile. Simon Templar was most adept at dealing with normal circumstances by abnormal and inventive means. He knew in advance of the light beams' existence, and he came well-prepared to deal with them.

The thermal bodysuit he wore under his overcoat and the matching hood pulled over his head were not intended as fashion statements, and the probe wired to it served a singular and important purpose. He passed the probe under the lowest bar and noted the digital reading off his wristwatch as the probe tracked his rising body temperature. At the exact instant his temperature matched that of the corridor, his watch emitted a delicate beep. He then took one well-measured breath and passed undetected through the beams of light.

Five minutes later Simon Templar was enjoying one of the more outstanding elements of his outlaw artistry—safecracking. In his earlier days Templar relied on tactile sensitivity and an amplified microphone placed near the dial on the safe door. He would listen to the distinctive clicks of the inner mechanisms, translate the sounds into numbers, and simply dial in the proper combination.

Today, however, he used a technological marvel built to his own exacting specifications—the Safecracker. Digital in design and battery-powered, its tiny arm worked the combination lock while an internal processor analyzed myriad sequences in rapid succession.

Templar set a small explosive cap in the corner and checked his watch. He glanced at the wall-mounted security camera, then at a Watchman receiving transmission from the small video camera he had planted in the lobby. It clearly showed the images appearing on the lobby's security monitor: a steady succession of fish-eye views of the Tretiak building corridors, stairwells, and offices. If he had gauged the video sequence correctly, he had six seconds before the safe room would be flashed on-screen.

"Precision timing," Simon whispered to himself through cheek pads and false teeth. He removed the Safecracker and hugged it to his chest, moving directly under the security camera. When the safe appeared on the lobby monitors, everything looked secure. Moments later Templar and his high-tech assistant were back at work.

As the Safecracker whirred and clicked, the downstairs business conference was building in intensity. Ivan Tretiak himself was glad-handing the attendees while Yuri Vereshagin prepared the lighting and atmosphere for his boss's important address.

Ilya paced impatiently. He had heard it all before, seen it all before. Ivan Tretiak was his father. Ilya didn't feel overshadowed; he felt eclipsed. Besides, he had an important meeting of his own nagging for attention. He headed for the door, but Vereshagin intercepted him.

"It is poor manners to walk out on our guests," hissed the fiercely loyal Vereshagin.

"Would you prefer that our leader's son pissed his pants in public?" countered Ilya. He pushed his way out and strode purposefully down the empty hallway as if he were an important young man late for a big meeting.

The young Russian skulked into the service stairwell. His big meeting was with a vial of methamphetamine. He spread the noxious powder on the back of his hand and sniffed.

His head rocked back as if he had been pleasantly punched, his eyes squinted, and he shook away the burning pain in his sinuses. He laid out another line, but just as he leaned down to snort it, a gust of wind blew it away.

Aggravated, Ilya complained under his breath.

"Why the hell is there wind in a stairwell?"

He looked up. The landing's window had been forced open. Ilya growled and took a closer look.

On the top floor the Safecracker finished its concerto of metallic whirs and clicks. The safe popped open, and Templar reached within and removed a black box the size of a cuff-link keeper. Inside, cushioned on velvet as if it were a precious stone, rested a gleaming microchip.

He slid the chip into his breast pocket as an unexpected outburst of angry Russian sliced through the silence.

"Stoyat! Ruki za golovu!"

"Sorry, mate," said Templar in his best Australian accent, "I don't speak the language."

"In that case: Freeze. Put your hands behind your head."

Templar complied.

"Turn around, slowly."

Templar swiveled to face his adversary—Ilya, armed with a Smith & Wesson 66.

The high-strung Russian gestured toward the dark hood covering Templar's face.

"Wrong place for a condom. Peel it off."

The burglar obliged.

The armed henchman took a good look at the intruder's face—a creative combination of technically augmented putty and prosthetics.

"God, you are one butt-ugly bastard." Ilya laughed with a cruel bark. "Who the hell are you?"

"Saint Uniatz the Inebriate," replied Simon pleasantly, giving Ilya an obvious looking-over, "Patron Saint of the fashion impaired. You must be my next case."

Caught off guard by the burglar's attitude, Ilya was momentarily confused. He clenched his jaw and stared intently, extending his empty hand. "The microchip, please."

Templar noticed something telltale in the Russian's movements, the twitch of his facial muscles and, most of all, his pupils.

"Listen," said the burglar reasonably, "I give this back to you, Daddy locks it up again, what do you get? Not even a Christmas bonus. On the other hand, you go fifty-fifty with me, a half million dollars in hard currency, you could buy all the Methadrine in Moscow."

Ilya, surprised, ignored the accurate reference to his drug of choice.

"You've got nothing to bargain with," he countered, and waved the pistol as if handguns settled everything. "Why don't you just give me the microchip before I shoot you?"

"As opposed to?"

"Shooting you first and then taking the microchip."

Templar reached into his breast pocket, pulled out the precious item, and began toying with it. He rolled it between his fingers as a magician would a coin.

"Give it here!" Ilya barked.

"You'll get it, don't worry, but first you can answer one quick question."

Ilya cocked his head in disbelief.

"You're gonna ask me a question?"

A crooked smile distorted the burglar's twisted visage.

"What did Simon Magus do in Sumaria?"

As the words were spoken, Simon flipped the chip into the air toward Ilya. The thug's eyes searched in desperation, and his weapon wavered. In that split millisecond, Templar moved with the force of a compressed steel spring, kicking Ilya full in the head.

Ilya reeled from the impact, falling, his Smith & Wesson clattering to the floor. He was quick to retaliate with an expert leg sweep, bringing Templar down. As Ilya scrambled to retrieve his gun, Templar pulled a radio transmitter from his pocket. Closing his eyes, he pressed the button just as Ilya's hand closed on the gun butt.

The explosive cap planted in the corner burst forth in a hot-white phosphor flare, filling the room with blinding light.

Templar ran like hell.

He raced back through the corridor toward the stairwell, violating the heat-seeking light beams, setting off alarms, and triggering a succession of unflattering photographs from a series of closed-circuit cameras. Ilya followed, cursing, blinking away the flare's retinal afterburn.

As for the man who would never again be called John Rossi, there was nowhere to go but up. Fighting blustery winds on the rooftop, Templar sprinted to the balustrade.

As he gripped the rail, a blast from Ilya's Smith & Wesson blew away a chunk from beneath his fingers.

"Give it up," ordered Ilya. "It's either that or fall ten floors."

"Easy choice," responded Templar, and he vaulted over the edge.

Shocked, Ilya rushed to the stone railing.

Peering over the edge, the stunned Russian saw the ugly intruder free-falling through space to certain death. Ilya didn't wait to see the impact. He ran back for the microchip.

Ever efficient, Templar used the free-fall time to discard the padding from inside his cheeks, spit out the teeth, pull off his mustache, and discard the putty appliqués before hitting the bed of a truck parked at the curb. He bounced as if from a trampoline and landed feet-first on the sidewalk.

Templar's truck; Templar's giant air bag on the truck bed.

Restored to his natural look, Simon reached into the truck's cab and pulled out a ragged knee-length overcoat and peasant headgear.

While the escaping Saint was altering his identity, Ilya was on his knees in the safe room searching for the flipped microchip. His fingers found it, but a closer look revealed it was nothing but a button from the burglar's bodysuit.

The stream of expletives unleashed by Ilya would, if printed herein, offend even the most sophisticated reader. Suffice it to say, the man was overwhelmed by anger.

Below, a cadre of security emerged from the building alerted by the numerous alarms. Rather than run, Templar lurched at them, palm outreached as if for a handout. The guards rudely pushed him aside.

Ilya, now accompanied by two other henchmen, blasted out the door of Tretiak Industries with his mind on fire. Fueled by adrenaline and Methadrine, he nervously snapped at the men from lobby security.

"Where's the body?"

The security guard had no idea what Ilya was talking about.

"Body? All I've seen is some guy in rags."

Ilya's peripheral vision captured a scraggly bum rounding the corner at the end of the block. Alarm bells rang in Ilya's head, and he took off after him.

Templar hurried through an archway and passed a convoy of Russian troops. Directly ahead of him were thirty pro-Tretiak demonstrators proudly marching and waving placards. He immediately joined their ranks, shouting slogans and working his way to the front of the parade.

Ilya and his men ran faster than the procession marched. When they saw the bum moving to the parade's head, they increased their speed even more.

Templar dodged out of line and into the Red Square crowd. He pulled a vodka bottle from his overcoat and quickly linked arms with a genuine bum who was more than surprised to find himself suddenly joined in generous, jubilant camaraderie.

Searching for the illusive lone bum, Ilya raced past the two joyous drunks. Templar then gifted the vodka to his grateful acquaintance, ducked into a doorway, and reversed his coat. He now appeared attired in a brightly colored parka. Then, from the right-hand pocket, he retrieved a cap fitted with long hair.

Ilya's eyes scanned the crowd of demonstrators and sightseers. Typical tourists snapped photos of St. Basil's cathedral. And then he saw him—a lone bum moving hurriedly toward Ilyinski Street.

With lightning-quick strides, Ilya caught up with him and spun him around. The ragged man clutched a half-empty vodka bottle as if it were his baby.

"It's mine! You can't have it!"

31

Wrong bum.

Infuriated, Ilya stomped off. He paid no notice to the tourist in the loud blue parka snapping pictures of the CNN correspondent and her crew broadcasting live from Red Square.

Ilya looked up at the giant video screens. There was his father, Ivan Tretiak, larger than life and twice as loud.

"Russia is riddled with criminals, hoodlums, and bandits," ranted Tretiak via video projection to the enraptured crowd, "shake-down artists, exploiters, carpetbaggers, and sports-car-driving capitalist opportunists! Where does this come from? Hollywood! And you know what lies beneath the fake tinsel and glitter of Hollywood? Real tinsel and glitter! But is Hollywood your enemy?"

Half the crowd yelled *"Da!"* Half the crowd played it safe and waited.

"No!" yelled Tretiak. "Your enemy is inside the Kremlin taking orders from the West to perpetuate the heating crisis!"

The international news cameras sent Tretiak's message around the world.

"President Karpov sits in the Kremlin, a silly puppet of Western Imperialism and . . . and . . ." he searched for an appropriate cultural buzzword, "capitalistic family values!"

The mob stamped their feet. They were very cold.

"Yes, stamp your feet! Stamp your frostbitten feet!"

The thunder of a thousand feet filled the frosty air.

"Now, if you can stop stomping your feet and chattering your teeth, you can throw President Karpov out of the Kremlin!"

Overwhelmed by Tretiak's manifest logic, the crowd stomped even louder.

Simon Templar did not remain in Red Square long enough to enjoy the conclusion of Tretiak's speech, but he watched it replayed on the first-class video screen aboard his British Airway's flight to London.

The in-flight recap of international news featured a disturbing montage of Russian unrest, frozen bodies being removed from buildings, President Karpov ducking rocks and bottles, and a point-counterpoint exchange between Ivan Tretiak and Russia's elected democratic leader.

"How can NATO talk so boldly of expansion to the East?" asked Tretiak from the front steps of his elaborate Moscow mansion. "They must have a secret understanding with Mr. Karpov. Whereas it is we Russians who should be expanding—rebuilding our great Soviet empire, by force if necessary."

"If Mr. Tretiak persists in accusing me of collusion with the West," countered President Karpov from his Kremlin office, "he must produce proof of his scurrilous claim—documents, correspondence, hard evidence. If he cannot, then I demand that he stop the demagoguery and call off the dogs!"

The broadcast completed, other passengers then tilted back their seats, pulled little blue blankets up under their chins, and availed themselves of tight black eyeshades. The elegant young man in the luxuriously tailored suit, however, sat idly swinging a gold chain with an antique locket in front of his face. It was as if he were trying to relax by hypnosis.

The well-tended matron sitting across from him couldn't resist initiating conversation.

"For a special someone?"

He handed her the locket, offering an inviting smile to go with it.

"Ah, cloisonné," she said coyly, "made by Byzantine monks, I suppose. My husband says that men only buy their wives jewelry when they're cheating . . . so I say . . . cheat, cheat, cheat!"

They both laughed as if her remark was a joke rather than a blatant invitation.

"I'm Irena."

Templar admired her warmly before speaking in an authentic Central American accent.

"Martin. Martin de Porres. I was named for a Panamanian saint who could instill new life by the laying on of hands."

"Really?"

3

SCOTLAND YARD WAS THE NAME GIVEN TO THE FIRST headquarters building of London's police force in 1829 because the rear entrance of the building was on the site of a 12th-century palace used for visiting Scottish royalty.

The headquarters was moved in 1890, again in 1967, and was now officially New Scotland Yard, although most people continued calling it by its original name.

Scotland Yard maintained criminal records for the entire United Kingdom and had a Special Branch, akin to the Secret Service. It also maintained close links with Interpol.

The Yard was famed for its detectives, including the portly, phlegmatic investigator known for his demeanor of perpetual boredom—Chief Inspector Claude Eustace Teal.

Inspector Teal came from a long line of short detectives with boring features. He joined the force in his early twenties, pounded a beat like any young copper, and earned a reputation for plodding efficiency, if nothing else.

But there *was* something else. Perhaps because of the plodding, perhaps due to dedication, Inspector Teal always got his man. Hence, his promotion to chief inspector.

Teal had none of the theoretical scientific training in criminology with which the new graduates of the Police College were pumped to offensive overflowing, but he had a background of thirty years' hard-won experience.

The droopy-eyed detective's reputation was the stuff of legend. Any criminal learning Teal was on his trail cringed at the prospect of certain incarceration— any criminal, that is, except one.

As a general rule, Inspector Teal was not concerned with matters of international diplomacy. The squabbles of world leaders, in-fighting of revolutionaries, and tiffs between terrorists were seldom issues of professional concern unless such misbehavior took place within the confines of London.

He was always willing to offer complete cooperation to Interpol, or any other such agency, when directed to do so by his superiors. He was especially prone to add an extra measure of dedication when personally prompted by Sir Hamilton Dorn of Special Branch, or the commissioner of Scotland Yard himself.

It was precisely such a situation that found Inspector Teal standing in the commissioner's office, clasping a bowler hat over his protruding stomach.

"Have you been following this Russian situation, Teal?"

"I watch the news," replied the detective. "Seems they're having a spot of trouble."

The commissioner plucked at his mustache.

"A spot of trouble, indeed. Sit down."

Teal sat.

"I don't need to tell you that Her Majesty's government is, in the most official manner, supportive of President Karpov's democratic reforms. The situation there is unstable at best, and should Tretiak and his October Party take over . . ."

He let the sentence hang before tossing several surveillance photos across the desk.

"MI5 has been watching Tretiak like a hawk, and it seems there was a rather daring and very peculiar robbery at Tretiak Industries—and the M-O is all too familiar. They think it's your boy."

The expression "your boy" was one Teal had grown to resent. It signified a particularly aggravating individual whom Teal had, without success, been intent on capturing for more than eighteen months.

"I wish you wouldn't use that expression, sir," said Teal wearily. "The name on his file is *The Saint.*"

"That's why they think he's your boy," continued Teal's superior. "He identified himself as Saint somebody or other when Tretiak's security tried to nail him."

"He always does that," added Teal, "and then he escapes."

"Of course," confirmed the commissioner, "he always escapes, he always uses cutting-edge technology, he always . . ."

Teal didn't need to hear the rest. He knew it by heart. There was only one uncaptured criminal in the world who fit the description being delineated point by point.

The dour detective examined the photographs of a heavily disguised Simon Templar racing down the halls of Tretiak Industries. He placed the photos on the commissioner's desk and began rotating his hat between his fingers.

"And what did our Saint make off with this time?"

"Some fancy microchip, but that's not the point. British Intelligence believes he's operating out of the U.K., and I don't mind telling you that we're suddenly under a great deal of pressure to bring him in so Special Branch can"—he pulled harder on the mustache—"have a word with him."

"A word with him, sir?" Teal looked bored, but he was keenly interested.

The commissioner leaned back and continued pulling. A small bare patch was beginning to manifest itself above his lip.

"As long as he was stealing diamonds, paintings, corporate secrets, and other such nonsense, it was a different matter—"

"Excuse me," Teal interrupted, "what's different now?"

"Politics, Teal. It's one thing to lift an authentic Van Gogh from a Netherlands museum, but quite another to rob that crackpot Ivan Tretiak himself, right in Tretiak's own building, right in the heart of Moscow. That means your boy has been in contact with prominent players in this Russian situation. What he knows, who he knows, could be of significant value to British Intelligence."

Teal considered the implications with thoughtful intensity.

"Well, Her Majesty's government doesn't like Tretiak," observed the detective, "the Yanks don't like Tretiak, and every other democracy in the West doesn't like Tretiak. For all we know, British Intelligence hired the Saint just to make Tretiak's life as miserable as he's made mine."

The commissioner let out a long laborious sigh.

"Sir Hamilton Dorn rang up just a few minutes ago. He thought maybe the CIA was behind it, but it turns out they thought we were behind it. I just got off the phone with Interpol as well."

Teal rotated his hat three more times before speaking.

"I've had it out with Interpol about the Saint on several occasions. Believe me, sir, we all want to catch the Saint, or at least find out exactly who he is and who he works for, although my impression is that he works for himself."

"Precisely," agreed the commissioner. "Tell me, Teal. Do you have any solid leads, any real suspects, or . . ."

Inspector Teal slowly unwrapped a stick of spearmint gum, folded it into his mouth, and began working it slowly.

At length, before the commissioner could become impatient, he shared his closely held personal opinion.

"I've seen every type of thief you can think of, from the small-time hood to the big-time operator, but I've never before come up against anyone like the Saint," admitted Teal.

"Obviously," said the commissioner.

Teal ignored the negative implication.

"Most criminals have egos so big you almost have to reserve a separate cell for their self-image," explained the detective. "They love to sign their crimes just as if they were artists painting a masterpiece. Same with the Saint. Except . . ."

"Except what, Teal?"

"Except there is something off-kilter about him, I mean as far as criminals go." Teal's cheeks turned pink. "He is incredibly impudent."

"Impudent, you say?"

Teal nodded.

"I almost had him once, you know," insisted the detective, becoming almost animated. "I was face-to-face with him within minutes after the Prince of Cherkesia incident. I admit I didn't realize it was him at the time, but he actually had the nerve to take his index finger and poke me repeatedly in the stomach!"

The commissioner stopped pulling his mustache and stared at Inspector Teal.

"He poked your stomach?"

Teal realized how ridiculous he sounded, and his cheeks almost glowed from chagrin.

"Well, let's leave my stomach out of this," offered Teal.

"Please," urged the commissioner.

"That episode gave me my only direct contact with the Saint—at least as far as I know," the detective explained. "He checked into the fanciest hotel in all of London, wore the most convincing disguise you ever saw in your life, and proceeded to run a multimillion dollar scam on one of the biggest insurance companies in the U.K."

The commissioner squinted, as if scrunching his eyes would aid his memory.

"Oh, I recall, I recall," intoned the silver-haired official, "the one we later indicted for denying beneficiaries their rightful claims."

"Exactly, sir. That's what I'm getting at. Every so often he pulls some stunt entirely criminal but . . ."

"Justified?"

Teal would have squirmed were he the squirming type, which he was not.

"I wouldn't go that far. Crime is crime."

The commissioner thumbed through a file on his desk. A particular notation caught his attention, and he tapped the page with his forefinger.

"Tell me about the phone call."

Teal did not like discussing the phone call because it required him to say something nice about Inspector Rabineau, and Teal would rather not mention Rabineau at all.

"The Saint—and we're sure it was him—rang up Scotland Yard about six months ago, right after he looted the Essenden Estate. Half the county constables were hot on his trail. . . ."

"Quite a merry chase from what I hear."

"Merry, indeed," Teal elaborated. "He jumped right off a rooftop into empty space and disappeared."

"The phone call." He put the detective back on topic.

"Oh. Yes." Teal cleared his throat and chewed with renewed vigor. "Apparently, while he was doing his best to elude the police, he crept by a flat, peeked in the window, and saw some fellow mistreating a child in a most cruel manner. He actually called Scotland Yard and reported it. Inspector Rabineau did the follow-up, and she managed to rescue that child from a most tragic situation."

"Sounds like your boy should be up for citizen of the year," mumbled the commissioner sarcastically.

Teal drummed his fingers on the top of his bowler.

"The point I'm getting at, sir, is this: We don't know who the Saint is, and I don't think he knows, either. He doesn't act like any sort of felon I've ever encountered before. But I will capture the Saint. He's bound to slip up because, sooner or later, they all do."

The commissioner stood from his desk and walked over to the window. He pulled a tiny comb from his pocket and began smoothing the wild hairs on his upper lip.

"It's not so much prosecution that we're after at this point, Teal," he said vaguely. "As I mentioned, there are international political implications involved. Your boy may have information that could be . . . invaluable. In truth, according to Sir Hamilton Dorn, the entire Tretiak theft smells fishier than a boatload of kippers."

"Sir?"

"No one messes with Ivan Tretiak and lives. No one even tries. In other words, either someone or some nation is exceptionally daring and inventive—the Japanese perhaps—or it was an inside job. Either way, the Saint is in the middle of some pretty nasty business."

Teal looked at the clock. As a rule, meetings with the commissioner seldom lasted this long.

"I'm assigning Rabineau to work with you on this one, Teal."

The detective almost choked on his gum.

"Rabineau?"

"She's the best of the new breed. . . ."

"So she says. . . ." Teal mumbled under his spearmint-scented breath.

"There's a fresh batch of composite sketches of the Saint in action around the world from Interpol, plus that latest one from Russia. If he's on his way back to London from Moscow, you have ample time to make it to Heathrow."

The commissioner turned from the window and put away the comb.

"We want to intercept the microchip, bring him in with it, and turn them both over to MI5. Don't detain a likely suspect simply for a questionable passport. We want him, *with the chip,* dead to rights. Is that clear, Teal?"

It was clear. Too clear.

"About Rabineau, sir. Have you briefed her on—"

"The political aspect? No. You're a chief inspector, she's not. I think you two will make an excellent team."

And that was that.

When the door behind him closed, and he made his way to his tiny, cluttered office, Chief Inspector Claude Eustace Teal of Scotland Yard sat down and deposited a fresh stick of spearmint gum into his mouth.

"Politics and Rabineau," muttered the detective, "two good reasons to take early retirement."

Simon Templar was not surprised when diligent customs officers at Heathrow Airport thoroughly ransacked his bag. They also compared his piratical profile to the recently transmitted images of a certain fleeing burglar audacious enough to violate top-level Russian security.

"Nothing personal," offered an officer, "but this is

4 3

the first flight from Moscow since the 'incident,' and you're about the same height as this gent."

Simon examined the fuzzy photo of himself in hasty retreat through the corridors of Tretiak Industries.

"He does look a bit like me . . . in the advanced stages of demonic possession."

Bored, Templar turned to a mirror which he knew was one-way glass. He could easily guess who was watching from the other side. His guess was, of course, accurate.

Chief Inspector Teal of Scotland Yard stared at Templar's face, and almost believed that Templar was staring back. Which, in a way, he was.

Teal turned his attention to a row of computer-generated composite sketches. Each sketch showed a different man, yet there was something naggingly familiar about all of them.

The detective's pudgy finger poked at a sketch from last year's heist of the Perrigo diamonds. The mere fact that the Perrigo diamonds were illicit to begin with, and Perrigo himself a notorious diamond smuggler, didn't alter the illegality of the heist.

"Same chin structure, you notice that?"

He spoke to Inspector Rabineau who, by her own assertion, was one of Scotland Yard's best trained and most astute detectives. She carefully considered Teal's observation, then offered one of her own.

"And look at the sketch from the Reuban Graner incident in Tenerife—"

"I thought that was Haiti."

"No. Tenerife, Canary Islands . . . same eyes."

On the opposite side of the glass, Junior Inspector Desmond Pryke arrived in customs with a fresh X ray of the detained traveler's innards. He held it up to the light.

"If this is the culprit," said Pryke, "he didn't swallow the microchip."

Simon shrugged and stole a glance at the high-contrast display of his gastrointestinal system.

"The salmon mousse looked so much lighter during dinner. Have you quite finished?"

A furrow-browed functionary examined Simon's authentic-looking but completely fabricated British passport.

"Ian Dickerson . . . ?"

"Yes," affirmed Simon cheerily. "I was named for the Canadian saint who first imported peanuts to France."

"That so?" The official, unimpressed, returned the passport.

"Indeed, he eluded the British authorities for decades." Templar added the irrelevant detail as if attempting to earn extra points on a quiz program.

The three custom officials stared blankly.

Behind the glass, Teal and Rabineau continued consulting their panoply of criminal portraits.

"You know, Teal, this fellow is a dead ringer for the perpetrator behind the Brass Buddha theft, except for the hair and the nose. . . ."

"Did you say 'and the nose' or 'in'?"

The droll Chief Inspector, his round pink face set in its habitual mask of weary patience, transferred a wad of gum from one side of his mouth to the other.

He leaned over to take a closer look at the portrait in question.

"Could be, could be. Also a resemblance to the Count of Cristamonte. Damn. Hard to tell."

Teal unwrapped a fresh stick of spearmint gum.

"I want to be absolutely certain," he insisted. "We can't afford to make a mistake, not now. If he's our man, criminal pride will catch up with him. He'll think he is immune to capture, get sloppy, give himself away, it always happens sooner or later. It's as predictable as liturgy . . . except . . ."

"Except what?"

Teal frowned gloomily.

"Except right this minute we have absolutely nothing we can pin on him, nothing at all."

Rabineau, not having the benefit of the commissioner's briefing, became impatient.

"We could detain him for investigation," she asserted with insistent passion. "He looks suspect to me, and he could be traveling on a forged or fraudulent passport!"

"I'm not going to endanger potential prosecution by playing a weak card like that," stated Teal succinctly. "If he doesn't have the microchip, we can't take him in."

She scrunched her nose as if Teal were emitting an unsavory odor.

"Besides," added the detective for justification, "I've received directives from our superiors regarding handling of this matter."

Rabineau's jaw tightened and she leaned into her superior's personal space.

"Am I out of the loop on something here, Inspector?"

Teal sighed. He answered without looking at her.

"Afraid so. Higher-ups sparring with other higher-ups. You'll get used to it before you get over it."

He could sense her resentment at being excluded.

His attitude softened, for he was, above all, a good man.

"Politics, Rabineau. The commissioner, Sir Hamilton Dorn, Special Branch, MI5 . . ."

He said plenty without really saying anything.

Rabineau smirked.

"Oh," she said flatly, "I guess that settles that."

On the other side of the glass, Simon Templar smiled, lifted his luggage, and watched his fellow departing passengers strolling unmolested toward the exit. Among them was the ripe and willing Irena. Bouncing above her ample bosom was the Byzantine locket.

4

SIMON TEMPLAR SAW BOTH THE BOSOM AND THE LOCKET again less than an hour later in a plush, deluxe, and dimly lit hotel suite.

Martin de Porres, alias Ian Dickerson, had fully demonstrated the Saint's technique of hands-on rejuvenation, and Irena was not disappointed. She reclined in repose as Simon gently stroked her shoulders.

"We know you have a choice when you fly," he murmured affectionately. "So, we thank you for choosing . . . us."

Irena laughed easily, and the locket bounced like a tuppence on a trampoline. Templar took it in his hand.

"The locket hangs a bit low. It calls undue attention . . ."

"To my 'generous bust'?"

"Generous indeed," acknowledged Simon.

"Are they out of date? My husband says only small breasts are in these days."

He examined the bosom objectively.

"Like fins on a Cadillac, a classic style is always appreciated."

Simon pulled a small penknife from his pants pocket and motioned toward the locket.

"Let me remove a few links for you."

She obligingly unclasped the necklace and handed it to him before starting toward the bathroom.

"Don't be long," called out Irena with a wink, "and I won't be, either. I'm just going to slip into something less visible."

When Irena reappeared from the bathroom, she was wrapped in a thick terry-cloth towel showing a perfectly modern hint of cleavage. The man she knew as Martin was not there to appreciate her ample charms. He and the locket were gone.

"Cheat, cheat, cheat," said Simon Templar to himself as he exited the elevator in the hotel lobby, pried open the locket, and removed the microchip.

He unsentimentally tossed the broken locket into a nearby wastebasket and placed the microchip in an envelope.

It may be said that our Saint of multiple personalities was a man of singular purpose. Having achieved his goal of securing the microchip, all that remained was delivery and payment.

It had been two and a half weeks since the staff of London's elite Belgravia-Copeland Residence Hotel had seen Mr. Orseolo Bodenheimer. A shy Italian of mixed ancestry, he was an exemplary tenant and true gentleman who paid his rent in advance and never caused trouble.

The moment he stepped from the large black taxi outside the hotel's beveled glass doors, the lovely Jamaican night manager recognized the shuffling gait of the slightly stooped and studious-looking man who maintained a simple suite on the second floor.

"Mr. Bodenheimer," she called warmly, "always a delight to see you, sir. I trust you're well."

Speaking with a slight Italian lilt, he handed her an envelope.

"Would you please overnight it to Mr. Miyaki at this address in Tokyo?"

She nodded pleasantly as an eager bellhop, new to the hotel, bustled over to grab the resident's bag. The night manager, knowing their guest's habits and wants, subtly restrained him and offered a whispered explanation.

"Mr. Bodenheimer was named for a sainted Santa Cruz bibliophile who left his family to pursue a life of *solitary* contemplation."

She put the emphasis on *solitary,* and the bellhop understood her to mean "leave him alone."

The respected recluse spoke generalized evening greetings in idiomatic Italian, and the bellhop watched his potential tip disappear up the stairs.

Inside his understated Georgian-style suite, Orseolo Bodenheimer's shuffling gait and stooped posture miraculously disappeared. A few moments later, gone also were the fake eyelids, false nose, and wig-hat. Simon Templar was now simply himself, the one identity with which he was not completely comfortable.

When he applied makeup and costume, he was a

man of his own design—limited in purpose, disposable as the lighters flicked in Moscow's Red Square.

There had been a time when he defined himself as a joyous, swashbuckling crusader for justice, but that heroic self-perception died in a Hong Kong orphanage a quarter century ago.

The hero of his reckless youth, Knight Templar, had bequeathed to him only a name—one name among many—and a bravado exterior polished and refined through practice.

Having removed his disguise, Templar checked his awaiting phone messages. As with his other high-tech toys, the answering machine stored messages originally received by numerous phones in diverse countries, and intended for several distinct identities.

"This is Galbraith Stride calling," began one angry caller, "and I'll be hanged if you think—"

Simon pressed the delete key.

"I think; you should be hanged," muttered Templar.

Countess Anusia Marova called to complain that she couldn't find her yacht, and Simon smiled knowingly before deleting her as well.

Templar raised an eyebrow at the sound of George Kestry of the NYPD calling to confirm tickets to the Detective Endowments Association's annual fundraiser, and he laughed aloud at an entrepreneur's enthusiastic request for several million dollars to bankroll a "Conquest of America" tour for Grand Theft, a has-been rock band from the 1970s.

The balance of the messages were couched in tones either seductive or vindictive, depending on the caller's gender and how recently they had discovered a sudden absence of family heirlooms, precious stones, or negotiable bearer-bonds.

He glanced around at his DBS television system, infrared remote controls, Power Pentium laptop PC, and a wardrobe of astonishingly expensive suits. If his boyhood hero wore chain mail and steel, this Knight Templar preferred armor forged of cashmere and silk.

Simon Templar had no illusions of altruism, romance, or selfless service. Too brave and mighty to be merely a rebel without a cause, he was a Templar devoid of king or crusade.

He was also without regrets.

"I may not know *who* I am," admitted Templar to the mirror, "but I know *what* I am—the first great outlaw of the twenty-first century."

He spun from the mirror and grabbed the television remote, wielding it as one would a pistol. He surfed through fifty channels in half that number of seconds, pausing briefly to watch a scene from an old black-and-white detective movie starring George Sanders. The debonair cad was cracking a safe by using only deft touch and focused concentration.

"My, my," murmured Simon, "this must be the educational channel."

The TV went dark in favor of a turbo-powered laptop with wireless modem. Within moments Templar was accessing the National Bank of Geneva's private accounts site.

The laptop's screen filled with detailed information of his personal Swiss bank account. A long column of deposits, each in the range of one to three million, gave him a combined total of slightly over $47,000,000.

He drummed his fingers impatiently on the keyboard and glanced at the sweep-second hand on his custom-crafted watch. It was time to be paid.

He waited.

The figures suddenly rearranged, and the screen reflected a new deposit and a revised total: $49,000,000.

"Can't seem to break fifty million," said Templar aloud as he shut down the laptop. He punched a button on his universal remote. A CD changer automatically selected something by Mahler as Simon stripped for a quick shower.

Towel-dried and freshly scrubbed, Simon slid into black silk pajamas and returned to his laptop.

Too tired to sleep, Templar began browsing cyberspace for his next high-yield heist.

"When I reach fifty million," he once promised himself, "I'll retire right out of sight."

The area of the Internet habitually visited by Simon Templar was not one usually glimpsed by the casual web-surfer. The access numbers to many of these bulletin board, ftp, html, and http sites were far from common knowledge.

Speeding along the Criminal Infobahn, he suddenly hit the brakes and pulled over. There was a single item on a page all its own. Simon leaned closer and read slowly.

DOES HUMAN FLY WANT TO EARN MORE FLYPAPER? GIVE ME A BUZZ. BORIS THE SPIDER.

Russians?
Templar logged on as "Human Fly" and began to respond.

IF YOU LEAVE ONE MILLION DOLLARS ON DEPOSIT, THEN I KNOW A ROMANTIC LITTLE SPOT IN BERLIN CALLED 'TEMPLEHOPF' WHICH HAS A COZY LITTLE TRANSIT LOUNGE.

In reality, the Communist bloc architecture of Templehopf airport was stark and devoid of inviting ambiance. To get inside, everyone had to walk through metal detectors. It was, therefore, cozy only from the standpoint of personal safety.

Simon Templar, dressed as an aristocratic young German, passed easily through the detectors to mingle with international business types, cut-rate tour groups, and a bevy of Nordic beauty queens on their way back to Bergen.

He scanned the crowd for signs of "Boris the Spider." He saw nothing. On guard, his jaw was tight.

Then he heard something.

Laughter.

It was the laugh of one small, curly-haired girl whose innocent giggle was as bright and crisp as summer morning wind chimes. For that moment, Simon was far away. His face softened, the jaw relaxed, and an honest smile almost touched his lips.

The little girl's mother grabbed her hand, reprimanding her in some foreign tongue. As the child was dragged from view, Templar instinctively turned away.

He was face-to-face with Ilya.

The Russian looked him over carefully, trying to decide if this aristocrat was the same man who eluded him in Moscow. Simon helped him out by making a face and puffing out his cheeks.

Had they been in a cartoon, Ilya's jaw would have clanged noisily to the floor while his eyeballs shot rocketlike from their sockets. Instead, he merely gulped and, clacking a walking stick, briskly backed up several steps to where another man sat reading the comic section of *The International Herald Tribune*.

The man admiring the funny pages was Tretiak, the

megalomaniac orator and would-be ruler of the New Russia.

Tretiak folded the funnies, set them on the table, and stood to greet Templar.

His handshake was firm, but quick to release.

"It's always a pleasure to meet a man so skilled in any profession. But tell me, Mr. . . . uh . . . Fly, for whom do you work? CIA or MI6? Some multinational corporation, or a terrorist state perhaps?"

The response was curt but accurate.

"I work for me."

"Good," said Tretiak with a thin smile. "Then no one will complain if I kill you?"

"Well, my investment broker will be devastated," admitted Templar, and Tretiak chuckled.

"We could kill you and stroll away, even here in this transit lounge . . . but"—the Russian pretended to weigh options—"today, I wish to hire you instead. Allow me to buy you coffee?"

Simon allowed. Ilya followed behind like a trained Doberman as they strolled to the food service.

Templar allowed Tretiak to buy the coffee, and he also allowed him to do the talking.

"That's a marvelous microchip you stole from me. It could regulate oil flow, pressure, which pipeline . . ."

"Everything except artificially inflate the prices?"

"The human element is, as you note, required for certain specifics," continued Tretiak. "The Japanese are miffed at having to build a new prototype. I mean *really* miffed—you'd think we invaded Manchuria again."

"What do you mean 'we,' Boris?" asked Simon, reinforcing any emotional distance between them.

Tretiak laughed like a wheezing pig.

"My name, as you know, is not Boris. I am Tretiak, but I assume you are familiar with my face."

"I've seen it on television. You were in Red Square saying rude things about Hollywood."

"Yes, a terrible corruption of the arts. . . ." Tretiak stopped, pondering perhaps whether he was being teased. "But enough talk of degenerate American influences."

Simon cast a glance at Ilya. "Speaking of which . . ."

Tretiak suppressed a wince. "Ilya is my son, a good son. He follows orders. Hence, I love him dearly."

"How totalitarian of you." Templar smiled. "I wish you much happiness."

Ilya paced and glared. He clutched his tapered walking stick, tapping out an irritating tattoo on the pavement.

Templar eyed him casually. The young Russian walked gingerly—*too* gingerly—and free from limp or other infirmity requiring cane support. As Ilya's fashion sense was no more highly evolved than his critical thinking abilities, Templar rightly regarded the stick as a deadly weapon rather than style accessory.

Tretiak renewed the conversation.

"I assume you saw today's newspaper."

"The headlines or the comic section?"

Tretiak forced a grin.

"The headlines were all about me, my call to Russian rearmament, and my new nationalist movement."

Templar shrugged. "Politicians bore me."

"Very well. We will get down to business. Do you know what cold fusion is?"

"Of course," replied Simon. "It's an imaginary form of nuclear fusion at room temperature. Cheap, free energy forever."

56

"Exactly," Tretiak confirmed, and this time his smile was genuine.

Templar shook his head. "As science, cold fusion ranks right up there with astrology. Those who claim to have achieved it have never seen their experiments duplicated."

Tretiak's face took on an air of triumph. "Until now, my daring friend, until now. There is a Dr. Russell working at Oxford . . . a woman . . . very difficult. She has made a breakthrough. Your job will be to obtain her formula."

Templar allowed his eyes to look off into the distance as if pondering a price. He knew his price before he passed through security.

"Three million dollars."

"Ridiculous!" Tretiak balked.

"Really? A monopoly on the world's energy? It's less than a nickel for every million you'll make."

Tretiak pretended to reconsider. He knew he would agree to the price before he left home for Templehopf.

"This is not for us," said Tretiak. "It is for Mother Russia."

"My bank account is in Mother Zurich," countered Templar.

The game completed, Simon provided Tretiak with an account number for deposit. The Russian handed Templar three pages of sparse typewritten notes about Dr. Russell of Oxford.

"This woman," added Tretiak, "is not going to be easy to get close to. Many of our best agents have repeatedly tried to befriend her. They all failed. She is very cagey."

"Perhaps," suggested Simon as he prepared to leave, "she simply has immaculate taste."

He started to stroll away, but stopped and turned back.

"Oh—the chip I was hired to steal from you. It's in the possession of a Mr. Miyaki . . . supposedly."

Tretiak lifted his hand. Between his fingers was an identical chip.

Templar smiled. "I assume I passed my audition."

"*Sayōnara,*" replied Tretiak, and Simon Templar vanished into the crowd.

Ilya stomped over to his father, demanding an explanation. "What if I had killed him in Moscow?"

"I would hire someone you couldn't kill," answered Tretiak dispassionately.

Ilya's face reddened. "What if he had killed *me?*"

Tretiak put an arm around his wayward son. "He was instructed *not* to kill you; it was part of the job."

The boy didn't know whether to be relieved or dismayed.

"Come, Ilya," instructed Tretiak. "Our thief has gone to work, and so must we."

5

THE MID-TWELFTH-CENTURY UNIVERSITY TOWN OF Oxford, a city of 115,000, was situated fifty-five miles northwest of London in the heart of Oxfordshire, England, where the River Thames joins the Cherwell River.

Students and townsfolk co-existed in contemporary ease, but clashes between town and gown killed many students in the fourteenth century. In the sixteenth century, three students were burned at the stake for their opposition to the Roman Catholic church. None of them, of course, were made Saints.

While Oxford was no longer infamous for violence and disorder, campus events continued to generate significant media coverage by journals and magazines catering to a wide spectrum of specialized interests.

Displaying credentials from *Scientific American,* eccentric investigative reporter Roger Conway ventured from London to Oxfordshire for the singular purpose of investigating Dr. Emma Russell's controversial claims regarding cold fusion.

The balding journalist was running slightly behind schedule when he nervously arrived at the Oxford science building. Well-dressed researchers and a handful of scientists sat informally around a room which was half laboratory and half lecture hall. They listened in rapt attention to an academic woman of sixty drone on about matters scientific and obscure.

Conway, doing his best to not disturb the proceedings, quickly sat down behind an exceptionally attractive young woman.

As he seated himself, she took a small pill from a bottle and swallowed it.

"Excuth me mith," lisped Conway softly, "can I have one of thothe?"

"They're for my heart. I don't suggest eating them like candy." She was, at least, courteous.

He took her hand and the bottle to check the label. He was lucky she didn't slap him.

"You're a very pretty lady," Conway said as if it would be news to her. It wasn't.

Her nose crinkled in mild, ill-concealed disdain.

"Who are you . . . exactly?"

For a moment, the "exactly" almost threw him.

"I'm Roger Conway, a writer for *Thientific American*. I have to interview Dr. Ruthell—expothe her for the fraud thee ith."

The woman looked quizzical. "Thee ith?"

"Yeth."

She blinked, shook her head, and turned away.

The journalist pulled a pencil and small notepad from his pocket.

"You don't buy any of thith cold futhion mumbo jumbo, do you?" The pencil was poised to record her response.

She ran her eyes over him as if he were gravel and she was a monster truck.

"Actually, I do."

The boring academian at the podium ground her introductory remarks to a much anticipated climax.

"It is, therefore, my privilege to introduce our guest today—our visiting research fellow and the foremost expert in the field—Dr. Emma Russell."

Conway nudged his reluctant acquaintance. "You ever theen Ruthell before?"

"Every day, first thing in the morning," replied Emma Russell, and she stood up to take the stage.

Despite being in disguise, Simon was mortified. Thankfully, no one noticed that the sudden blush of his cheeks did not spread to his fake bald head. Everyone's eyes were riveted on Emma Russell's simple, exquisite beauty. Everyone's, including Simon's.

Emma began quietly, awkwardly.

"I didn't really prepare any special remarks. Maybe I should just take questions."

A student put up his hand. She nodded at him.

"Dr. Russell, can you please explain the actual process of fusion—the theory of it?"

"Sure." Emma smiled, warming to the subject. "Thermonuclear fusion usually depends on high energies, but the possibility of low-energy, low-temperature nuclear fusion is, I believe, about to become a reality. Back in 1989 Stanley Pons of the University of Utah and Martin Fleischmann of the University of Southampton first described their cold fusion experiments . . ."

An enthusiastic student couldn't contain himself.

"Isn't that when they immersed palladium and platinum electrodes in deuterium?"

"Yes, exactly," confirmed Dr. Russell. "When positively charged deuterons in seawater are attracted to a palladium cathode, they cram together—millions of them, inside the cathode, clustering with no place to go until . . . they fuse, creating energy in the form of helium. Lightning in a bottle."

Simon Templar had little or no interest in cramming deuterons. Emma, however, was a different matter.

Another student spoke up.

"Various laboratories around the world have tried to duplicate the process, but with generally negative results. If the experiments can't be replicated, how do we know it works?"

"We don't," admitted Emma. "Not yet. But Einstein knew relativity to be true long before he could prove it. He saw the vision of it—saw its truth. Some of us feel that way about cold fusion because it's there in nature. The raw natural power, waiting to be harnessed. More energy in one cubic mile of seawater than in all the known oil reserves on earth."

Templar was enthralled, and not with the subject matter.

"And when we finally ignite that cold fusion fire—imagine!" Emma's mounting enthusiasm was contagious. "You could drive your car fifty-five million miles on one gallon of heavy water. It would be the end of pollution. Healing for the wounded earth."

She turned to the blackboard.

"Here, let me demonstrate why others have been so unsuccessful in the past."

As Emma Russell began expository drawings, the bald man in the back slipped out the door.

Outside, Simon Templar laughed aloud at his own foolishness. He seldom made embarrassing mistakes, but he readily acknowledged this one. A minor consolation was knowledge that Oxford's history was replete with people who had acted foolishly. Among them was famed poet Percy Shelley, expelled in 1811 for publishing *The Necessity of Atheism.*

While Templar did not share Russell's near religious zeal for cold fusion, he did share her dedication to thorough investigation. He returned to his car, slipped on a pair of coveralls, and searched out Emma Russell's personal office.

"I'm Tony Hubbins from Tech Support," said the working-class Brit to Russell's distracted collegiate assistant, Trish, as he walked through the doorway, "named after the patron saint of quality footwear."

"Good," she replied without looking up. "You know where I can find shoes on sale?"

He walked directly over to the office computer and stared at it as if he could see into its inner workings.

"This baby has a short in the motherboard, I hear."

The assistant checked her fingernails for any new chips from excessive keyboarding.

"It was working an hour ago—I used it myself."

Templar began disconnecting the tower drive.

"Dr. Russell 'erself called," he explained as he lifted the tower and started for the door. "You'll have it back by the weekend."

"Take your time." The assistant yawned. "There's nothing on it 'cept the first chapter of her book on exotic piscapology."

"Erotic who?"

She rolled her eyes. "Fish."

"Oh."

The patron saint of quality footwear put one foot in front of the other, exited the office, and took the tower with him to a nearby Oxfordshire inn, where a rented room awaited him.

Trish was absolutely right—there was nothing on the hard drive concerning cold fusion, but plenty about fish.

Tony Hubbins promptly returned the tower, offering Trish his assurances that everything now worked perfectly.

Later the same day Templar easily and illegally entered Emma Russell's mid-Victorian faculty-row apartment. His intentions were less than honorable, and even he felt a slight twinge of regret that even $3 million could not completely buy off.

Before a man can steal, he must lie—lie to himself that what he is doing is justified. At this stage of his lawless career, Simon Templar was a master of justification.

If Tretiak wanted cold fusion to reheat Russia for his own political ends, at least there would be heat. Didn't Dr. Russell want her theories validated, the world benefited? An easy justification, indeed. If he said these things to himself often enough, he could almost see himself as the patron saint of energy.

Browsing her apartment, he noticed books, plants, and candles were everywhere. There were Post-it notes plastered on the walls, and even a few on the ceiling.

He pressed the Playback button on her answering machine.

"You have no new messages," said the machine in a fair approximation of human intonation.

"She may be cute, but she's obviously not popular," murmured Simon as he picked up a postcard from the Shelley monument.

He moved to the crowded bookcase and thumbed through her extensive, eclectic collection. Scientific journals shared space with compendiums of poetry and a few literary surprises. *The Tao of Physics* rested against *The Promulgation of Universal Peace,* while *The Purpose of Physical Reality* was crowned by a worn, first-edition copy of *The Hidden Words of Baha'u'llah.*

He picked it up, opened to a random page, and read aloud softly. " 'The best beloved of all things in my sight is justice.' "

A small tingle crept up from the base of his spine, and he did his best to ignore it. He replaced the book, then continued on to the bathroom, bedroom, and sitting room.

In the latter a huge fish tank filled with exotic multi-colored fish dominated a corner. It was attached to a glass vessel identical to the lab apparatus Emma used when explaining cold fusion to the students. It buzzed quietly and appeared to be the tank's only source of energy.

Simon stopped his investigations to admire the beauty of Emma's exotic fish.

"I could watch you guys all day," asserted Templar honestly.

He moved into the kitchen where he found an improvised lab spilling liquid into the sink. Dr. Russell had adapted every kitchen implement to another task: weight scales, the garlic press, and the percolator had all been pressed into service to manufacture little brown granules which stood in a peculiar pile. The pile continued to grow because it was continually added to, drop by drop, from the spout of a teakettle.

Whatever it was, it was most unusual.

Templar walked to her desk and powered up her laptop computer. There was a bottle of Inderol lying by the keyboard.

Prepared to break her password code, Simon was astonished to discover that she didn't have one.

"No password? Emma, you are bold, refreshing, and a first-class nut."

He entered a few basic commands, and the backlit screen soon filled with equations, equations, and still more equations, interspersed with snippets of art and poetry.

He slipped in a computer disk and began backing up her hard drive. While files were transferring, he noticed receipts from the Trout Inn on her desk. Opening a drawer, Templar discovered her journal. Two photographs from the Shelley monument fell out, and he carefully replaced them before shamelessly reading her most personal thoughts.

Stop and talk to Shelley every day. How can I love a man called Percy Bysshe?

Templar turned the page.

Isn't there someone who can consume me like that? Oh, Lord. I am single, alone, and lovely . . . lonely . . . lowly?

Simon replaced the journal, his clever mind analyzing Russell data as if preparing to crack a safe.

Next to her bed was a photo of a young Emma with

a tall man, obviously her father. He wore long hair and a cardigan sweater. Templar could almost inhale the fragrance of musk- or herb-based cologne.

"Not a citrus sort," reasoned Simon, "but perhaps Gray Flannel."

He slipped a tiny camera from his pocket and snapped the father-daughter photo.

"Tretiak's wrong," Templar said to the fish. "She's not cagey, just innocent and eccentric. Those secret-agent types would strike out in a heartbeat."

He examined more of the Post-it notes on the walls. Most were snatches of poetry.

He sat down and attempted to soak up the atmosphere of her life, her environment, her identity. Despite being a scientist, she was a poetic sensitive with mystical yearnings.

A smile touched the corner of Simon's lips.

"Low-tech." Templar chuckled to himself. "This is a low-tech job."

Were Emma Russell a building to be burgled, a safe to be cracked, or a security system to override, it would not be accomplished by electronic gadgets and gizmos.

The road to Russell's research was through her heart.

Templar thought of George Sanders' safecracking scene in that old movie. He listened, he touched, he was sensitive to the subtle nuances.

Templar would listen with sensitivity, and gently turn her affections until all emotional tumblers were aligned. She would open; he would steal. Simple.

A sudden sound from outside sliced through his concentration and drew him to the window. Dr. Emma

Russell had exited her car and was heading directly toward the apartment.

Simon ejected his disk from the laptop. There was no time to leave, only to hide.

A key rattled in the door, footsteps entered, and an answering machine said there were no new messages.

Emma Russell walked past her fish tank while removing her blouse.

"I could watch you guys all day."

With mounting curiosity, Templar watched as Dr. Russell reached inside her bra and removed several business-size cards and placed them on the table.

She moved into the kitchen, pulling on a handy lab coat. She lit a scented candle, put on some music, then simply sat down in the corner chair with her eyes closed.

As for Simon Templar, had he not been well-trained in the art of silent movement, she would have spotted him long ago. She didn't even sense his presence.

He watched, he waited. A few minutes later she retrieved the cards from the table, opened her journal, and began to make notations.

In time Emma set her work aside and left the room. When Templar heard the shower running, he took advantage of the opportunity to vanish as if he had never been there. In truth, he didn't want to leave.

6

THE FOLLOWING DAY TEMPLAR PREPARED FOR HIS NEXT
encounter with Emma Russell. With his usual professional detachment, he selected a cardigan sweater similar to the one worn by Emma's father, dabbed a small
amount of rugged-scented cologne behind his ears,
and filled his head with poetry.

"If one is going to catch fish," Simon Templar once
remarked, "you must place the perfect lure in the perfect spot."

The perfect spot was the Shelley Monument; the
perfect lure was Templar himself. Having read her
journal, he knew how often she visited, and when.

He, a romantic figure with long, flowing hair, reclined on a bench, highlighted by sunlight. Purposefully languid and inviting, he began sketching
Shelley's statue.

When Emma arrived, she noticed him immediately.

After one look she could not pull her eyes away. She was simply and openly attracted. He was, after all, exceptionally handsome. He also reminded her of her father.

It was not out of her way to approach him, and he spoke to her without looking up. His accent was South African.

"Do you like it?"

Emma was momentarily taken aback. Was he speaking of the statue, himself or . . . ?

"The sculpture," clarified Simon. "Do you like it?"

She swallowed and did her best not to sound self-conscious.

"Yeah." She meant to say it nonchalantly, but it came out with a sort of squeak as if someone had stepped on a rubber duck.

Templar suppressed a laugh.

"What do you like about it?"

On this topic Emma could speak with confidence.

"The way it glows, the way the light holds him in silence, as if caring for him."

Her answer was beyond what Simon expected. He stood from the bench and said nothing.

Emma edged for an opening to continued conversation.

"That's what I like about it. Are you an artist?"

Templar smiled at the question, and his smile was authentic. Her directness and simplicity were having an unexpected influence on his attitude.

"There are no artists anymore," he asserted. "You must be pure, like Shelley. No, I'm nothing—just a traveler—but I do search for purity." He paused, but only slightly for effect. "What do you search for?"

"Energy."

It was such an immediate response that the word was out of her mouth before she had an opportunity to consider the question.

The young man projected an air of enticing, controlled enthusiasm.

"You must experience the energy of where life began—Africa. Have you ever been on a long journey?"

Emma looked down briefly.

"No," she admitted, "not ever, really."

Simon walked toward her with easy confidence and familiarity, as if he could sweep her up in his arms and cradle her like a child.

"Would you like to?" He stepped closer as he asked.

She stepped back, but not out of fear. Perhaps it was propriety.

"Yeah," she squeaked again, and a slight blush filled her cheeks.

"Perhaps I'll take you on an adventure to my home in Africa." He was moving closer still, but not in a threatening manner. Emma decided not to step back. Templar was close enough to kiss her. Wisely, he did not.

"I'm sorry if I am too familiar," said Simon shyly. "I apologize. I'm not very good with people." And with that bit of fabricated self-disclosure, he was gone.

Emma stood, breathless. His scent was intoxicating. Her senses seemed to tingle, and her heart—often an object of concern—seemed to be beating in perfect health.

She allowed herself to exhale slowly and turned to notice that the wondrous young man had left behind his sketchpad/journal.

* * *

"The lovely little fish," stated Simon to himself as he sat in the ergonomic comfort of his Volvo C70, "has taken the bait."

As a man who planned things perfectly, his selection of the C70 was no more haphazard than his approach to Emma. Simon's first car had been the famous Volvo 1800E. Hence, his purchase of the C70 was inevitable. His appreciation of fine automobiles was long-standing, especially those of distinctive style, legendary heritage, peak performance, or unparalleled safety. The C70 was all of the above.

He owned other vehicles as well, some of them non-descript and purely functional, placed strategically around the world. He also held title to several vintage classics, including a 1933 Hirondel, a Bugatti '41 Royale, and one of the last known Furilacs in existence.

Dr. Emma Russell, however, had no passion for fine cars. She bought her VW Bug because it was inexpensive and got her where she was going.

The little Volkswagen pulled up to her apartment. Emma exited and, lost in her own thoughts, walked to the entrance. She stopped, fished in her briefcase for a notepad, and began furiously jotting.

Drops of standard-issue U.K. rain began to fall, but Emma continued to scribble. The drops became a light shower. Having completed her sudden burst of note-jotting, Emma turned her open mouth to the sky and allowed nature to fill it with water.

Simon, watching, sighed.

Dusk dropped its backcloth behind Emma's apartment. Inside, she studied the young man's journal. Dr. Russell was fascinated by the drawings, the poems, the mind.

She searched for an indication of his identity, but there was no name, no address.

The following afternoon, beside the Thames, Emma sat at her usual table at the Trout Inn. The river view did not captivate her; 'twas the journal that held her enthralled.

Templar, of course, was there as well. Positioned where he would not immediately be noticed, he studiously avoided looking in her direction.

When Emma saw Simon, she snapped the notebook shut. Convinced that he had not seen her, she debated returning it. She opened it again and found something that caught her attention—a poem.

As poems go, it was not publishable material. Publication was not Templar's intention. It was verse aimed at the fragile, vulnerable heart of Dr. Emma Russell.

"And, when the showers of pure light dance in her clear eyes . . ." it began, and continued on its way to an awkward but well-intentioned conclusion.

Simon, choosing the moment, picked up his plate and approached her, reciting the poem aloud as he walked.

"We, purified by our kisses," he concluded romantically, "are eternally healed."

Emma, a bit flustered and curious about the impurity afflicting the poem's kissers, told him it was beautiful and should be funded by National Health.

"Are you following me, or is it destiny?" asked Simon. "Either way, it's weird."

"Weird as in 'fate,' or weird as in plain old weird?" Emma made space for him to sit, pushing his journal into the corner.

"Destiny. Pass the salt."

She complied and began the conversation.

"I can't believe I ran into you again. I can go weeks and weeks and never run into my friends."

Simon gave her a doubtful look.

"Well, I have two friends. Actually, one," confessed Emma. "I guess she's a friend—she knows who I am."

"A lucky woman," commented Simon.

Emma realized that the young man and she had never introduced themselves.

"My name is Emma, Emma Russell." She offered an exceptionally attractive hand.

"Thomas More."

"After the saint?"

"Sounds like a book title. Yes, Thomas More died for his faith. You know him?"

Emma hedged. She didn't want to offend her new acquaintance's religious sentiments.

"Not personally, I'm not that old. I've heard of him, though," remarked Emma in half jest. "As a kid I was bullied by nuns."

Simon's face involuntarily flushed, stinging as if Father Brennan had slapped it only moments ago.

"The nuns I knew were kind, thankfully," he honestly responded, "but Father Brennan . . ."

He stopped himself, disbelieving his own hears. He had not uttered one word about his experience at St. Ignatius since he was thirteen years old. Why now? Why here? In the middle of what should be a smooth, simple, well-rehearsed deception, truth was an unwelcome intruder.

Sensing discomfort, Emma changed the topic by pulling three or four cards out of her clothing. Templar recognized them as the cards she previously extracted from her crowded brassiere.

"Crib sheets for the Rosary?"

"No, silly, it's something I'm working on. A formula for creating energy."

"Try eating chocolate and drinking coffee," suggested Simon helpfully.

"Not that kind of energy. Are you teasing me?"

He nodded in playful affirmation.

"Are you a student, then, Emma?"

"I was a student, once, Thomas," answered Dr. Russell. "I am a research scientist."

Templar had palmed two of her cards. He laid them out with a slight flourish.

"Hey, how did you do that?"

"Magic."

Emma laughed, but disappearing cards were no joke.

"Give them back, please."

He passed them to her, along with his warm, wonderful smile.

"I just wanted to watch you put them away again. What else do you keep in there?"

"Nothing anyone has been particularly interested in," said Emma honestly.

"You know that's not true."

The moment was saved from embarrassment by the welcome intrusion of the Trout Inn's waiter.

"May I get you anything else?"

"The Latour '57," answered the romantic poet.

The waiter cleared his throat.

"The Latour '57, sir, is four hundred pounds."

"Per bottle or per glass," asked Templar without smiling.

"Bottle."

"Good price! We'll take two," he enthused and

pulled a handful of crumpled bills out of his coat pocket.

The waiter ambled off to fill the order, and Templar turned to Emma with a slight shrug.

She shook her head in amused disbelief.

"Perhaps I should have ordered the Latour '58?" Emma laughed.

"No, I'm sure the '57 is best, but you'd better be very thirsty."

He realized he should have consulted her before ordering.

"You don't . . ."

"Drink? No. Not often. Hardly ever, actually." Her cheeks flushed with self-consciousness. She didn't enjoy discussing her medical problems. "I take medication for . . . for my heart, to tell the truth. As a chemist, I am quite familiar with drug interaction precaution number 101. Inderol and alcohol don't really mix. Besides, Allah forbids it."

Templar, alias Thomas More, apologized.

"I'm sorry, I didn't know you were Moslem. I wouldn't have offered—"

Emma laughed sweetly and touched his hand, held his hand.

"I'm not really Moslem, although I could be. I know as much Koran as Catechism. My father was an orientalist much along the lines of E. G. Brown of Cambridge. You've heard of—"

"Cambridge? Of course," replied Simon with charm.

"No, I meant Edward Granville Brown, author of *A Year Amongst the Persians.*" Emma was trying not to giggle, and succeeded by her next sentence.

"Anyway, my father and I were very close. He

died—his heart—actually, he was struck by a car, but the heart attack killed him, although I blame the drunk behind the wheel. I was in my teens when it happened. I don't know if you have ever lost anyone close to you . . ."

Simon thought of Agnes reaching for him, falling . . .

He discarded his plans to ply her with expensive wine. He was, for the first time, feeling somewhat ashamed of himself.

When the wine arrived, he drank; she politely sipped. Even in measured moderation, Emma deemed the Latour '57 remarkably intoxicating. Perhaps the effect was more attributable to the ever-increasing charisma of her romantic companion. Either way, they were soon holding hands across the table.

Both pretended not to be thinking of kissing.

"Can I tell you something?" Emma asked.

"Will it embarrass me?" He was already feeling chagrined.

"No. Unless you don't like to be trusted. My energy research: It's done. Well, sort of, almost, nearly."

"Marvelous," said Simon. "I have no idea what your energy research is, but I'm pleased for you."

"Someone should be," commented Emma, "considering I was practically run out of America for pursuing this project."

Simon's expression prompted an explanation.

"The concept is called cold fusion. The entire idea is not taken too seriously back home in the good ol' USA, and it reached the point where I couldn't get any more research funding."

"So?"

"So, I still don't have any sort of fund or trust or

grant paying to develop my research. But I do have a little lab in my apartment, a supportive staff at Oxford, and I give several lectures a week—that pays the bills. Plus," she added, "I love England."

He knew she was minimizing and being modest. He liked that.

He eyed her and she eyed him.

It was as if there were searchlights behind her eyes, and he was trapped in their illumination with no dark corners to melt into, no false-identity alleyways to dart down.

He felt vulnerable and exposed, but stayed in character.

"Thomas More?" She pondered his name.

"Yes?"

"That's not your real name, is it?"

The room seemed to shift beneath him. Her next words echoed as if bouncing from the high ceilings of St. Ignatius.

"I think you didn't like your name, so you made one up."

He was incapable of immediate response.

"You were an orphan, maybe?"

She may as well have hit Templar with a baseball bat. He was astonished, but kept his reaction in check. The expression in his eyes, however, confirmed the accuracy of her assessment.

Emma Russell leaned dangerously close to him and squeezed his hand.

"It's okay. I'm an orphan, too. Mom died when I was three, and then Dad. I've been pretty much on my own since my teens. I'm just damn lucky I was born with brains and instilled with morals. Otherwise, who knows?"

Simon knew the otherwise.

It was difficult for Templar to recall **that** he had initially approached this job with heartless, cynical materialism.

"Have you done any research," asked Simon, deftly changing the subject, "on the romantic effects of warm chocolate?"

His phrasing was almost erotic. Emma's pulse quickened.

"Is it safe," she asked in jest, "to mix cocoa and Latour '57?"

He smiled a conspiratorial smile and ordered them each a steaming cup of hot cocoa topped with a dollop of real whipped cream.

"You look lovely with a mustache," intoned Templar.

Twenty-five minutes later she was almost dragging him into her apartment. When Emma applied herself to a project, she saw it through to consummation. She hadn't had a boyfriend, a lover, an anything, in ages.

"Welcome to the new age," said Emma cryptically as she led Simon into her apartment. He pretended he had never seen it before.

She set the mood, lit the candles, and put on music as if she were preparing for a scientific demonstration.

"Now what?" asked Templar with a touch of innocent curiosity.

"Trust me, I'm a doctor," advised Emma, and she told him to take off his shirt.

As he complied, she began to unbutton her blouse.

"What, exactly, are we going to do, Doctor?"

Emma tossed aside her blouse.

"First things first, Mr. More. I suggest we lay our cards on the table."

She removed the cards from her bra and placed them on the table.

"I'm not wearing a bra, and I have no cards," said Simon with the sweetest smile.

"But you have something up your sleeve just the same, Mr. More," responded Emma playfully. "Besides, I just want to look at you."

"Look to your heart's content."

Emma's eyes suddenly widened as if remembering something important.

"Oh! Thanks for reminding me." She grabbed her purse and dug inside for a small medicine bottle. "Hold that pose and hold that thought."

She moved to the refrigerator, opened it, and took out what appeared to be a beer bottle. She twisted off the top.

Standing there, bathed in the refrigerator light, she was a vision of eccentric, individualistic beauty, unpretentious, and thoroughly herself.

"Inderol and root beer," explained Emma wickedly, "a heady combination."

"I'll pass on the Inderol, but if you have two straws, we can sip it together in front of the fireplace."

Emma laughed, searched her cupboards, and found two straws. She placed them in the bottle.

"Light the fire, Mr. More, I'm feeling a chill."

"Shut the refrigerator," suggested Simon, and he built the fire.

As the dry logs began to ignite, Templar's eyes drifted to the cards resting on the coffee table. He was genuinely attracted to Emma and distracted by his primary objective—stealing the prized contents of her bra.

Together in front of the fireplace, sharing one root

beer with two straws, the fake Thomas More romanced the real Emma Russell.

"I'm not the kind of woman who brings strange poets home on a regular basis," said Emma as she seriously considered kissing him passionately on the mouth.

"Am I that strange a poet?"

She spared him an honest critique of his journal entries.

"I don't date much," confided Emma. "Most men aren't comfortable dating a research scientist who keeps file cards in her bra."

"You're my first scientist," said Simon comfortingly, "and the only woman I've ever known who used her brassiere as a file cabinet."

She leaned closer, setting the root beer aside.

"I'm not sure what it is about you, but you're different. . . . I mean, I'm different, too. . . ." Emma was becoming tongue-tied, and Simon helped her untie it with a kiss.

When their lips parted, she fanned herself with her hand.

"Whew! That's some fire you've built here, Mr. More."

They laughed, intertwined, disarmed.

More than anything, Simon wished he could level with her. "I wish I could tell you my story, everything about me."

"You could . . . you can. You don't have to hide. Really, it's very safe here in this little apartment. No one will know, except me and the fish."

"It's not as safe here as you think," stated Simon honestly. "In fact, it's very dangerous."

She snuggled closer.

"Oh, tell me about the danger," she teased.

"I might take from you what's most precious."

"A football player did that my senior year in high school," recalled Emma sardonically.

Simon looked at her lovely face. She was an authentic beauty.

"You are an authentic beauty," he said, as if having read the previous paragraph, "and I will treasure this night—"

"Till morning?"

He looked down with a penitent expression. "I'm not that kind of man."

There was a moment of tentative silence, augmented by the crackling fire and bursting bubbles of carbonation from the root beer bottle.

"Do you want to sleep with me, Mr. More?"

She was, at times, exceptionally direct.

"Exactly that," answered Simon, "I want to hold you close to me, and together we will sleep."

He wasn't kidding. She pressed her cheek against his. "You are a saint."

The warmth of her face increased the cold shame of his deception. He forced himself to ignore the unexpected feelings of regret and remorse rising within him, and pretended to sleep.

The following morning, Emma awoke and turned to kiss her saintly, chaste, and poetic lover. He was gone. Instinctively she raced to her cards on the table. They were not her originals. Each of the five cards read "I'm sorry."

Dr. Emma Russell brought her hand to her heart, felt it torn apart, and dropped devastated to her knees.

Tears flowed through her fingers and dropped in tiny splatters on the floor.

She felt more alone and betrayed at that moment than she had in her entire life. She sobbed and sobbed, and sobbed harder still, knowing that no one knew, and no one cared.

In the kitchen her makeshift laboratory spit out another pellet. In the fish tank her exotic pets swam in aimless circles. On the floor Dr. Russell continued to cry.

PART TWO

1

SIMON TEMPLAR DERIVED NO PLEASURE FROM STEAL-
ing Emma's cards, and the prospect of Tretiak's $3
million arriving in his bank account did not minimize
his sense of shame.

His rationalization, his only rationalization, was that
he had agreed to the job. He was obligated to deliver.

Templar digitized her cards and transferred their
images to his laptop. In a matter of moments Emma
Russell's life work was e-mailed to Moscow.

The reaction to its arrival was both enthusiastic
and lethal.

Tretiak had arranged for Russian physicist Lev Botvin to study Emma's work immediately upon delivery,
and the scene at Tretiak's mansion was one of elated
exuberance

"It's revolutionary, sir!" exclaimed Botvin, excitedly
wiping his glasses with his shirttail. "She's boldly cast

aside a slew of stale ideas . . . but it will take months of trials and experimentation before I can confirm—"

"That won't do," insisted Tretiak. "Now that the people are nicely beginning to freeze, Tretiak must sweep in from the wings with a miracle to save them!"

The wings of Tretiak's mansion were themselves in the midst of transformation. He enjoyed displaying his wealth in forms of conspicuous overstatement.

He led Botvin across a dropcloth-covered parquet floor awaiting a fifth coat of varnish, and passed between twin towers of wood scaffolding. Above them an extraordinary crystal chandelier hung from a pulley welded into the underside of the domed cupola. The chandelier's two massive wedding-cake tiers were stabilized by concentric rings of steel.

A workman shouted down from the scaffold.

"How high do you want this, Mr. Tretiak?"

"Not now, not now!" He waved impatiently at the workman, who shrugged and signaled his coworkers to secure it to a cleat bolted in the wall.

"Lovely chandelier, sir," commented Botvin with admiration.

"Screw the chandelier!"

"I think they did, sir," offered Botvin seriously as he peddled behind his leader.

Tretiak led him up to a fully stocked physics lab where Botvin began to nervously assemble the apparatus needed to bear out Emma's formula.

"Perhaps I can confirm the formula's validity more quickly if I dispense with certain protocols," began Botvin.

"Dispense with whatever you want," agreed Tretiak. "You will make cold fusion a Russian innovation, then Russia will command and the West will cringe!"

Botvin's glasses began to fog up again, and he looked askance at his leader in the process of wiping them. This did not go unnoticed.

"How long, Dr. Botvin, since your last salary check from Moscow University?"

"Ukrainian Independence Day," answered the physicist wistfully, "last August."

Tretiak chortled and threw an arm around Botvin's shoulders.

"Well, I don't foresee any problem in raising money for a man whose name will be synonymous with modern physics. The Lev Botvin Institute of Nuclear Fusion will be the greatest research facility any superpower's ever seen."

Had Botvin's chest swelled any greater, the little man would have either exploded or levitated.

The lab door swung open, and one of Tretiak's security men delivered a terse, yet important message.

"He's on-line, sir. Your Mr. Fly is on-line."

Indeed he was.

Simon Templar sat impatiently in his London hotel room, staring at his bank account balance on the laptop screen.

"C'mon, Tretiak," he murmured to himself. "Time for Boris to pay the fly."

The balance did not increase. Templar typed an urgent e-mail message to Boris the Spider.

Boris was sending Simon a message of his own:

RECIPE INCOMPLETE. CAKE WON'T RISE. HENCE, NO DOUGH.

Templar's jaw clenched. He banged out his reply.

I'M NOT THE BAKER—DON'T MAKE ME THE
BUTCHER!

Three blocks from the Belgravia-Copeland, Ilya
Tretiak edged his way through traffic. He drove another in his ever-expanding collection of imported
American 4X4 all-terrain vehicles. The fact that he
had never driven one on any surface other than well-
maintained pavement was irrelevant. To Ilya, appear-
ances were everything.

Accompanying him were two henchmen with high
foreheads and low morals—Vlad and Igor. Each was
ill-tempered, high-strung, and augmented by chemicals
best described as violent stimulants to the central nervous system.

The three thugs were not in the U.K. simply to test
drive Range Rovers or Jeep Grand Cherokees. They
carried an electronic triangulator keyed to the transmission signal of Templar's modem.

"How we doin'?" asked Ilya.

"Gettin' hot," Vlad replied. "We're almost on him."

"Good. If dear old Dad can keep him on-line long
enough, Mr. Fly will get the ultimate swat."

Igor choked out something resembling a laugh.
"Does that make us a swat team?"

"Yeah, an unofficial one, but a damn good one."

As Templar typed his next response to Ivan Tretiak,
Ilya and his two thugs further confirmed their
coordinates.

"There!" snapped Ilya. "Belgravia-Copeland!
Armor-up! Let's go!"

The three toughs screeched their 4X4 to an abrupt

halt outside the hotel, threw open the car doors, and marched toward the ornate entrance.

The Jamaican woman glanced out the window at their arrival and momentarily froze when she caught sight of ill-concealed automatic weapons.

Ilya led the way, stomping roughly into the lobby. Reanimated by the Russians' militaristic entrance, the woman reached for the silent alarm.

Ilya abruptly raised his silencer-equipped Sig-Sauer and squeezed off the one round that smashed through her forehead and terminated her life. He didn't bother watching her fall.

The bellboy descending the stairs was no more fortunate. Vlad finished him with a quick burst to the heart while Igor took control of the hotel switchboard. There were five lines in use, and he quickly monitored each one. Only room 17 gave him the distinctive whistle of a modem in use.

"Room seventeen," barked Igor, "there's a fax/modem on-line in room seventeen."

They took the stairs three at a time, raced to room 17, and kicked down the door.

Empty. Almost empty—a small transmitter sat on the floor, relaying Templar's modem signal from anther room.

Outraged and outwitted, Tretiak's three stooges spread out. They kicked open every door in the hotel. Terrified guests in various stages of undress screamed and shouted in fear and panic.

As Igor was about to knock down the door to Templar's actual suite, Simon was already on the ledge outside his second-story window. Below, a stately Bentley was moving past.

The driver, Dr. Terry Mannering, was lighting a

Spur cigarette when he heard the *thump* of Simon Templar landing on his roof. He raised an eyebrow and paused his carcinogenic inhalations. That was the extent of his reaction. He kept driving.

As Mannering turned the corner, Templar rolled off the Bentley and blended with the crowd surging across Sloane Square.

Ilya, Igor, and Vlad were compelled to admit failure. The Fly had flown.

As for Dr. Emma Russell, she could only cry for so long.

Her eyes were still red and wet when she related her tale of woe to Inspector Rabineau at Scotland Yard. Halfway through her tearful, rambling explanation, Rabineau abruptly interrupted her.

"Wait, wait, wait. He used the named of a *what?*"

Emma sniffled before answering. "Saint. He called himself—"

"Excuse me," interjected Rabineau. "I think Inspector Teal needs to hear this."

When the pretty blond American first arrived at Scotland Yard ranting about Shelley, a South African sketch artist, and a secret formula, Rabineau didn't consider the matter urgent nor Dr. Russell's story credible. When she mentioned the artist's alias, Rabineau's interest was significantly piqued.

When alerted by Rabineau, Teal lazily suggested that Dr. Russell be escorted to his private office. With both detectives in attendance, Emma began her story from the beginning. Teal insisted on hearing every detail, especially about the man who claimed he was named for a saint.

Emma revealed each embarrassing, humiliating particular, and dampened half a box of tissue in the process.

Her story completed, Teal and Rabineau exchanged glances. A nod from her superior encouraged Rabineau to begin.

"This man has more names than the phone book," asserted Rabineau. "We've confirmed a handful of false identities used on visas, passports, leases . . ."

She picked up a computer printout.

"Nicholas Owen, Louis Guanella, Peter Damian, Paul M. James, Charles Borromeo, Ian Dickerson . . ."

Emma leaned back and laughed ruefully.

"Of course, like 'Thomas More,' all names of saints or hagiographers."

"Hagiographers?" Rabineau squinted when she asked questions.

"Saint experts," explained Emma.

Teal cleared his throat and plopped another piece of chewing gum into his mouth.

"That's why we've named him the Saint," stated the detective flatly. "We have a name for him, and a criminal signature."

He spread out the numerous computer composite portraits and enhanced surveillance camera photographs.

"The Saint around the world," intoned Teal, "one crime after another, each in a different clever disguise."

He encouraged Dr. Russell to examine the 8×10 glossies of the Saint in action.

Emma surveyed the photos and her stomach sank.

"The Saint in New York, the Saint in London, the Saint in Miami . . ." Teal recited the captions in a droning litany.

Emma turned the last one on its side, hoping for improved clarity.

"I can't see the resemblance in this one at all."

Rabineau tossed down one from Heathrow. "Is this more like it?"

It was him, all right. No doubt.

Emma offered Teal the young poet's sketchbook.

"I doubt there's anything worthwhile in here. The poetry's not that great—well, there is one I like—but at least you have a handwriting sample and perhaps some fingerprints. I'm surprised he forgot to take it with him."

Teal flipped through a few pages, stopped chewing, and read aloud:

" 'To give light to them that sit in darkness . . .' "

Emma blushed.

Teal rolled his tired eyes and handed the journal back to her.

"He has multiple identities, steals millions of dollars, absconds with your life's research, and leaves behind his poetry. As evidence of anything, it's useless. I'm sure he knew that when he left it. You can keep it as a souvenir if you like, Dr. Russell. He may be a poet, but the Saint is no saint."

A sudden tingle raced along Emma's arms, and her eyes brightened.

"Excuse me," Emma said with an assertiveness that surprised even herself, "but could you ascertain the passenger list of every plane that left Heathrow in the last six hours?"

Teal sighed. "We'll be waiting for him if he ever attempts to reenter the U.K.," the detective assured her. "We'll have plenty of questions for him."

"No, I want that list, and I want it now." She was insistent. "Trust me. My objective is the same as yours—capture the Saint."

Teal complied with Emma's wishes and did not bother to mention that the odds of actually pinning any charges on the Saint were beyond remote.

The fingerprints left behind would match nothing in Interpol's database, nor would there be any way to prove that her sticky-fingered poet was an international criminal.

Dr. Emma Russell, armed with a passenger list for every flight from Heathrow, exited Scotland Yard and piloted her VW Bug back to the scene of the crime.

Teal masticated pensively as Rabineau paced.

"We don't have a damn bit more than we had before," mumbled the portly detective. "We have one more crime, if you can call taking notecards from the nightstand a crime fit for Scotland Yard. We have a suspect we can't identify, about whom we know absolutely nothing, and upon whom we can pin even less."

Rabineau stopped pacing, shuffled through the photographs of the Saint at large, and waited for Teal to add something to his negative assessment of the situation.

"Of course," added Inspector Teal, "we'll catch him, prosecute him, and see him sentenced to Wormwood Scrubs by year's end."

Rabineau doubted it, and Teal knew it.

"Defrock the Saint," said Inspector Teal while attempting to smile, "that's my ambition: defrock the Saint."

"Saint, my arse!" Rabineau blurted.

Teal adjusted his tie and cleared his throat.

"Beg pardon, Inspector." Rabineau pulled an imaginary wrinkle from her freshly pressed skirt. "A Saint he ain't. He's just another rat. A tricky rat, but a rat nonetheless."

2

"MAY THE BEST RAT WIN!" BELLOWED AN INEBRIATED Tretiak, and a dozen large rats began racing on a neon-lit mini-track in Tretiak's private club.

Rat racing had not yet become the rage in Russia, but it was the entertainment of choice in Tretiak's lair. American-style cheerleaders shook pompoms under flashing lights while well-fed rodents scrambled in a frenzied dash. Money flowed like wine, and wine flowed like wine as well.

Tretiak, always able to either pick a winning rat or create one, pocketed more hard currency as his guests drank up booze and felt up dancing girls.

"How is it you always win, Ivan?" asked a jovial General Leo Sklarov as he tasted the perfume behind a Georgian beauty's ear.

"It's simple!" exclaimed Tretiak. "I back the biggest rat!"

Everyone within earshot laughed as if it were the funniest remark since his previous remark. It wasn't, but he was rich.

Even the wealthy, rude, and powerful must surrender to certain inevitable weaknesses. Tretiak's well-lubricated digestive system was under more pressure than the second-run rat.

He excused himself, stumbled across the dance floor, and entered the rest room as the maître d' distastefully herded rats into a burlap sack and carried them back to the service entrance.

A nondescript man awaited the rats.

"Bring these filthy vermin back tomorrow night at ten," instructed the maître d', "and you're welcome to them."

Simon Templar took the rats and nodded compliantly.

Tretiak, looking a bit flushed, emerged refreshed from the rest room and stumbled happily toward his table.

"General Sklarov," called out Tretiak, "have I proved to you my brilliant theory that two singles don't make a double?"

"What theory is this?" The uniformed lecher laughed as he squeezed the Georgian's proprietary padding. "If it involves alcohol, it must be very important."

It was, as theories go, an easily demonstrated lesson in modern marketing. Tretiak had been drinking doubles, Sklarov had been downing singles while matching Tretiak drink for drink. Both men were thoroughly polluted in body as well as in morals.

Tretiak tossed his bottom down into the chair and wagged one finger at the glasses in front of him.

"You just watch and see," he slurred with authority and summoned a waiter.

"Pour two singles into that double's glass!"

The waiter complied, and the excess liquid ran down the side of the glass and soaked into the tablecloth.

"See!" Tretiak laughed and pointed. "Two singles don't make a double!"

Confused, Sklarov insisted the experiment be repeated.

It was, several more times for everyone at the table. Each round, Tretiak's party drained their glasses before the waiter renewed the experiment. Soon, everything was soaked and everyone was sloshed.

"C'mon, my little latka," called the drunken would-be dictator to his sozzled female companion. "Now I will show you a very special rat!" He laughed as if obscenity and wit were synonymous.

She giggled her most obligatory giggle and, gathering up her imported purse, joined her powerful lover. Sklarov, unconscious in his chair, did not even wave good-bye. His date was in the ladies' room hugging a toilet.

Tretiak steered his young lovely through the crowd, out the door, and toward his black BMW. They crawled inside, shut the door, and sat back to await their driver.

A large gray rat leaped into Tretiak's lap as two more yellow-toothed rodents jumped on his screeching and screaming girlfriend. Rats were everywhere, swarming over the seats and headrests, scampering over their bodies, and sniffing at their private parts.

Tretiak gasped and flailed his arms wildly. His panic-stricken date violently kicked her high heels at the swarming vermin.

Kicking, screaming, stomping, shouting humans and squealing rats rebelled at one another's behavior in a moment of madness and mayhem. The street-side door was suddenly thrown open, and the two terrified passengers erupted into the street.

Immediately upon exiting the BMW, Tretiak was slammed against the vehicle by Simon Templar.

The Saint thrust a cellular phone in front of Ivan's face.

"Your accountant's on the line," hissed Templar. "Have him deposit my three million in Geneva."

Tretiak's first impulse was to balk, but a pointed pressure between his ribs altered his reluctant attitude.

"I'll cut you into sticky little bits with my carbon steel machete," Templar threatened.

Ivan swallowed his rage. Watching his girlfriend and several rats running off into the distance, he began barking instructions into the phone.

Templar smiled.

"Oh, yes, and tell him to add two days' interest at current mutual fund rates, estimated travel expenses from London to Moscow, and funeral costs for the two innocent people your stooges killed this morning."

Ivan glared. Templar pressed the blade harder. Tretiak complied.

"Thank you so much," said the Saint pleasantly. "Now I will be able to treasure my memories of Moscow. Get back in the car."

Not wishing to be impaled on Templar's machete, and unaware that it was nothing more than a pocket-knife, Tretiak slid into the BMW. He was immediately welcomed by an exceptionally large and ill-tempered rodent.

He angrily slammed his fist into the vermin's

twitching little face and burst back out of the car. The rodent, unconscious, did not pursue the relationship. The Saint was gone.

Templar's taxi arrived predawn at a remarkably shabby inner-city hotel. Even at this odd hour a ragtag band of women stood by the front door. They offered to sell either themselves or their possessions.

Templar approached the front desk. "Mr. Farrar, checking out."

They began to prepare his bill amid numerous distractions. Sensing it would be a while, Templar crossed the lobby toward the bar. He peered inside and was dissuaded from entering by the cluster of Party hacks turned dealmakers, pimps, and miniskirted "models."

He opted for the coffee shop. After escaping from Ilya, tracking down Tretiak, and playing with numerous rats, Simon Templar had a headache that would only increase if exposed to more mindless mayhem.

He ordered a cup of something resembling coffee and pulled a small aspirin bottle out of his pocket. He dumped two tiny pills into his hand.

"Aspirin and caffeine," said the female behind him. "A heady combination."

Emma.

Templar whirled to face her.

There was one moment of penetrating silence, followed by the unmistakable sound of a woman's hand slapping a man's face. Emma's hand, Simon's face.

Somewhere, in the distance, a Doberman barked.

He tried to pretend the slap never occurred, speaking to her as if they were at a church social. "I'm rather surprised that you found me, or bothered to."

"It wasn't difficult," enunciated Emma precisely.

"Two men with Saint's names flew from London to Moscow yesterday—one was named Isadore Bakanja. He was short, bald, and African. Not even you could manage that disguise."

Templar seemed to give the concept careful consideration.

"Vincent Farrar," continued Emma with set jaw and iron eyes, "seemed far more likely to be your current alias."

Templar offered a rueful grin. "Named after a saint who betrayed his best friend. You're right. So what?"

"I want my cards back. The ones you stole."

"Oh, those." He turned unconcerned back to his coffee.

She slapped the cup and saucer away with the back of her hand and slapped his face again on the upswing.

"Bastard!"

The waitress pretended not to notice anything.

"I'm a thief, Emma, I steal things," explained Templar. "If it makes you feel better, you can slap me again."

He didn't actually expect her to, but she did. Harder.

None of this was helping his headache.

They stood there then at the coffee counter. His face red, her hand sore, the counter wet with spilled coffee and littered with pieces of cracked saucer.

"I'll pick up the tab for this," said Templar to the waitress. She hurriedly brought him a can of Tab and a glass of ice. Both he and Emma involuntarily laughed.

"Who the hell are you anyway?" asked Emma, and the question seemed not the least bit rhetorical.

"Nobody has a clue—least of all me," Templar answered.

"Why did you steal cold fusion when it was free? If you would have simply asked me, I would have given it to you! You are so damn stupid."

Simon did not bother formulating a witty rejoinder. She was absolutely accurate and correct. He had been stupid and cruel.

"Whoever the hell you are, I saw something good in you. I felt happy when I was with you," insisted Emma as if attempting to process her disappointment and dismay, "and you are a liar and a fraud. Give me one good reason why you should steal from me!"

"I can give you three million reasons, all of them recently deposited to my bank account."

"So, you lied to me for three million."

"You lied to me, too."

Emma was stunned. "I did what?"

"You almost got me killed. The guy I stole the stuff for says it won't work."

"Fuck him!" shouted Emma angrily.

"I don't think you'd enjoy that," offered the Saint.

She eyed him through a mist of outrage. "You're right, I'd rather it was you!"

Emma made a signal, and three Russian police were suddenly all over him, snapping on handcuffs.

"You don't know what you're dealing with, Dr. Russell," insisted Templar.

"The tables have turned," declared Emma triumphantly.

Her triumph was short-lived. In the next second the cops handcuffed her as well.

"Yes, they have," concurred Templar. They were

dragged from the coffee bar, through the lobby, and out to an awaiting paddywagon.

Separated from her purse, Emma begged for her medications.

"My heart pills, please. You must leave me my pills!"

They ignored her and tossed them both into the wagon.

The door slammed shut and the van roared off.

"They didn't give me my pills," lamented Emma in the dark.

"They didn't have them, I do," stated Templar softly. "I palmed them in the bar, pocketed them while they frisked you."

The van took a corner and the two prisoners collided into each other.

"Oh, God!" cried Emma. "My heart . . ."

"Which pills? Which pills?"

"The little ones in the vial, the nitros . . ."

Templar painfully repositioned himself, contorted, and plucked the small brown bottle from his pocket.

"I'm getting out a nitro, take it easy. . . ."

Emma was not taking it easy.

"Just turn around, you'll be fine. Kneel, eat it from my hand."

The van swerved and Emma toppled to the floor.

She sobbed. Her chest hurt.

"Emma! For God's sake, find me! Take it!"

She crawled on the cold steel floor toward his outstretched palms. She wrapped an arm around his well-trousered leg and put her open mouth into his hand as if giving it the kiss of life. Her tongue found the tiny nitro tablet and she took it.

She allowed herself to loosen her grip on Simon's

leg, feeling the distinctive nitro rush move up through the top of her head, taking her chest pain with it.

The paddywagon hit a bump, and she fell backward on the floor. Templar threw himself down next to her. The light flashed in through slanted vents as the van swerved around another corner, and she saw Templar tearing at his shirt with his teeth.

"What are you . . ."

"Emma . . . can you see under my arm . . . a tiny pouch of scar tissue . . ."

Awkward with the handcuffs, but he raised his left arm.

"Inside is a rod, about three centimeters long. Can you see it?"

Not easy in the dark, but she could just make it out—a smooth, hairless ridge just beneath the hollow of his underarm.

"Pull it out with your teeth."

"I'm so sure," objected Emma.

"They're taking us to Ivan Tretiak. His ambitions fill cemeteries. Trust me: You'd rather put your nose in my armpit."

She didn't trust him, but she believed him. She buried her pert nose in his perspiring pit.

The paddywagon accelerated, swerved, spun around several more corners, entered the compound of Ivan Tretiak, and pulled up on a ramp leading below the mansion.

It was Ilya who awaited the van, eager to take custody of the prisoners. He impatiently tapped his walking stick as the first cop climbed out of the cab.

"The two came very quietly," said the cop. He grappled with his keys and prepared to open the van.

Tretiak joined them, beaming.

"Open the door, quickly. I want to see the prize catch of the day!"

The door opened. Empty. Almost empty—two sets of open handcuffs and a length of chain.

Tretiak grabbed Ilya's walking stick and whacked the cop over the head. The sound of cracking skull was loud, wet, and unpleasant. The cop did not hear it. He was dead before the first splatters of blood stained the van door.

The second cop froze where he stood, and Ilya looked in admiration at his father. Dad was always a man of decisive action.

"Close the city!" yelled Ivan Tretiak. "Kill him and bring her to me!"

"Yeah," added Ilya, and he felt powerful saying it.

3

TEMPLAR AND EMMA RAN DOWN THE WALKWAY OF AN
ice-slick tunnel. The walls were plastered with posters
of Tretiak as a Christ-like messiah. A police car
streaked by, and Templar dragged the bedraggled
Emma into an alcove, where he pressed against her
as if they were lovers.

When their lips parted, she spoke. "Kiss me again."

Another cop car approached from the opposite direction and slowed to watch them kiss.

"Why are they after me?" she asked, her breath
merging with his.

Templar held her close. "Tretiak, the guy who hired
me to steal your formula, owns this city—cops and all.
We're going to have to convince him he's got everything he wants from you."

Emma pressed against him with unexpected assertiveness. "What do *you* want from me?"

He kissed her again.

"Are the cards everything?" he asked.

"Yes."

"And the formula will work?"

"No."

"Make up your mind."

She broke the embrace and leaned against the tunnel wall.

"I still have to figure out the right order. But I am not going to give it to him."

"Emma, he'll find you—he found me and that's a hard thing to do."

She looked him over. She was attracted, but not trusting. Not yet.

"I found you, too. It wasn't difficult, don't fool yourself. You have what Inspector Teal called 'criminal pride,' and it's what makes criminals get caught— they get sloppy or egotistical or both."

He put his arm around her. "Am I that sloppy?"

"You left behind a sketchbook filled with your poetry and drawings."

Templar felt an authentic smile light up across his face. "I did that on purpose, that wasn't sloppy."

"Oh? What was it, then?"

"Ego," admitted the Saint, and she actually laughed.

Together, they made it quickly to Moscow's massive railroad station. Fifteen tracks served this travel center, and thousands of Russians passed through daily. While waiting to board, travelers could purchase Peach Vodka in a can and chocolate bars from numerous competing vendors.

Considering the early hour, Templar and Emma found the station surprisingly busy.

"Where are all these people going?" asked Emma.

"Probably to their country cousins' where they can chop wood to stay warm," ventured Templar, and he was probably right.

Vlad, the third leg of the triad death squad, was assigned this venue. He saw Templar and Emma enter, and made a quick call on his cellular phone.

While Vlad informed Ilya of the couple's location, Templar opened a storage locker and pulled out passports and money.

"How much time do you need to finish your formula?"

"I need a kiss," replied the nervous Emma.

"Concentrate. Concentrate. How long?"

"I can't say for sure," she stammered, "anywhere from two hours to—"

"Good," interrupted Templar. "Just enough time for me to get the passports together for us to get married."

Emma was incredulous. "Married?"

"Yes, I want you to be Mrs. Martin de Porres." He showed her a passport featuring a photo of him in disguise as de Porres.

"Are you Martin?"

"I was named for a Saint who could cure the sick by the laying on of hands."

He touched her cheek.

"You're not Martin?"

"No."

"Who are you?"

"I don't have a name." Templar turned back toward his locker.

"Will you have one when we get home?"

"I don't have a home. You do the science, Emma,

and I'll do the math. We'll sell the formula to the highest bidder and get rich. Then we'll see. . . ."

Simon Templar, a man who was already $50 million to the good, suddenly felt poverty stricken—when he looked back, Emma was gone.

His eyes frantically searched the crowd. There she was—racing across the ticket office, pushing through the morning travelers.

He ran.

Emma sprinted into the foyer toward the open door. As she passed a pillar, Vlad grabbed her by the neck. Her feet kicked at the air, Vlad's strong fingers gripping her white windpipe. Her heart pounded wildly, and a red mist surrounded her eyes.

Vlad pulled out his flick knife and twirled it toward her face. His thin lips pulled back to reveal several rotting yellow teeth. Emma was amazed to see those same teeth explode out of Vlad's mouth from the impact of Simon Templar's fist.

The force of the blow sent Vlad sprawling like a stunned rat, his knife clattering across the floor.

"Never leave my side again, Emma," insisted the Saint. She nodded dutifully, popped another nitro, and ran with him toward the side door as Ilya and Igor jumped from their Range Rover and stormed through the front.

The chase was on.

Emma and Templar smashed their way out the side door, veered left, and discovered they were on a dead-end street that terminated at a canal. In moments Ilya and Igor would be joining them.

"Oh, God!" cried Emma. "There's nowhere to go!"

"Yes, there is, and if you don't see it, neither will they!"

When the two Russian henchmen hit the street, the fugitives had vanished.

Igor and Ilya prowled up and down the sidewalk, peering into alcoves and alleyways. Nothing. Ilya stopped and sniffed the air as if he were a dog.

Directly beneath his feet, on a foot-wide ledge of ice, Emma and Simon perched precariously above the rushing arctic water. They inched along carefully, silently, dangerously.

The couple's movements were tentative, awkward, and each sliding step was fraught with fear. Emma's hand trembled, and her little brown bottle of heart pills slipped from her grip and rolled toward the water.

Templar snatched it, retrieved it, and tossed it to her. Then, in a moment's fraction, the traction disappeared beneath him. He fought for balance, but the effort was doomed.

Emma watched in terror as Simon Templar vanished into the ice-filled water. It took massive willpower to keep from screaming.

Ilya stopped when he heard the splash, hastened to the ledge, and looked over the side. All he saw was water and ice.

Emma jammed herself into a crevice where the old stone had eroded away. Her body shivered with cold terror. Her left ankle seemed clutched by death itself, and a quick glance confirmed Simon's deathly white hand wrapped around her like a strange claw.

The Saint, using Emma as anchor, stayed submerged in the frigid canal. With each passing second, his body seemed to fade away in terminal numbness. The only sensation he had of his chest was that of his lungs about to burst. Looking up through the murky water, he could make out Ilya's distorted features.

Ilya saw nothing, but noticed his foot soldiers in the distance. They were across a bridge, scouring the far side of the canal.

"They must have run in the other direction," growled Igor. "I'll get the Range Rover."

The Russian swore in English and hastened after Igor. No one was going to drive that car but him.

Emma moved out of the crevice, giving herself enough footing to bend down and help Templar get his head above water.

Breathless and blue, Templar gulped air and tried to send signals to his unresponsive body. With great effort Emma maneuvered him toward the canal ladder. He took each rung as if he weighed a thousand pounds, agonizing over each movement.

Out of the water, Templar shivered. Waves of delirium swept over him, and he fought to remain conscious.

"C'mon, gotta get you warm."

Emma watched Ilya's Range Rover cross the vehicular bridge. There was no way she and Templar could be seen from the bridge. She piloted her wet and wobbly companion toward an apartment house across the road.

"I know it's hard to move . . . but try, quickly, before they circle back."

The Range Rover was beginning to circle back.

Emma hustled Templar into the building's grimy lobby. Lime-green paint smeared over concrete and sparse remnants of wallpaper established the decor, while the thick odor of mold and mildew attested to a history of benign neglect.

The front door, on a cheap, heavy spring, slammed loudly behind them.

Emma jumped.

Outside, Ilya's head snapped to attention: *What was that noise?* He squinted through the driver's side window at the row of dilapidated buildings, allowing a presumptive sneer to crawl across his lips.

Templar, shivering and dripping ice water, waited with Emma in front of the elevator.

"You'll wait till Christ comes to Moscow," said a voice behind them.

The bedraggled couple turned and stared at a teenage tenant outfitted in miniskirt and heels. Her makeup was excessive, garish, and ill-applied. She looked fourteen at best.

"Elevator was made of mahogany. We used it for firewood. This was a nice place once, before I was born," she explained.

Templar forced himself to speak.

"We need to hide. We're not criminals. . . ."

Emma attempted to clarify the situation.

"Just people who . . ."

The girl shook her head. "You're not just people, you're Americans. He's soaked."

The squeal of brakes added a sense of urgency, and the young girl saw desperation in Emma's eyes.

"Mafiya trouble, right? They must have seen you come inside. . . ."

Shivering, Templar pulled a handful of soaked dollars from his pocket. "Money, I have money. Please . . ."

Her eyes darted from the forlorn pair to the front door. She battled her instincts for survival and made a gut-level decision.

"I'm Sofiya," she said, and her tone was considerably kinder. "Follow me. Forget about the money . . . at least for now."

She herded them to the stairwell and encouraged them to start climbing. She and Emma helped Simon navigate the nine tiring flights to Sofiya's huge communal apartment.

One massive room, it had been cheaply subdivided with thin plasterboard to accommodate several separate families.

Despite his mounting delirium, or perhaps because of it, Templar could clearly discern the distinctive smell of stale coal smoke, the residual redolence of burned wood, and the pungent scent of laundry soap.

Sofiya tiptoed inside, trying to sneak the two Americans through the door unnoticed. No such luck.

A haggard woman with sharp features, deep-set eyes, and long dark hair tied back in a bun confronted the trio.

Emma quickly extended her hand in a polite gesture, but the woman ignored her. Her attention was focused solely on Sofiya, the immediate recipient of an emotional outburst.

Templar, trembling in his soaked clothing, understood every word. Emma, although not fluent in Russian, sensed the essence of the diatribe.

"Meet my mother," said the teenager, ignoring the woman's verbal barrage and expressive hand gestures. "She doesn't approve of what I do, but she eats the bread it buys. Too bad it can't buy more heat."

With Sofiya's mother muttering behind them, they continued on into the cluttered and chaotic kitchen. A riot of tattered clothes were hanging on makeshift clotheslines; one half of the double sink was filled with laundry, the other with dishes. The minimal heat came from one source—an old oven's open door.

A potbellied man sat at a 1950s-style kitchen table sipping kvass from a jar. A tiny ancient lady at a samovar—an authentic animated matrushka doll—looked up from stirring strawberry jam into a glass of black tea.

The man, seeing Templar drenched to the skin, let out a low whistle and a gruff laugh.

"Look at the polar bear! Took a dunk in the Moscow River on a bet?"

"Hush, Uncle Fyodor," admonished Sofiya, "he needs our help."

The old woman clucked her tongue in sympathy, and offered tea.

"Chai?" she trilled.

To Simon Templar, the entire environment seemed surreal and hallucinatory. The room appeared to alternately expand and contract, distances were inconsistent, and the reality of his own physical existence seemed questionable.

The elderly woman handed him the glass, but his shaking hands and feeble grip made the warm liquid spill out over his fingers. She wagged her head in disapproval, took it back, and began drinking it herself.

Sofiya hurriedly plucked clothes and towels off the line and handed them to Emma. Then, smiling sheepishly, she removed a hundred-thousand ruble note from her bra—the monetary rewards of her unfortunate vocation—and hung it on the line as payment for the items. Her mother looked the other way and crossed herself.

"The bra is a good place to keep valuables," said Sofiya.

"I know exactly what you mean," concurred Emma.

"I'll show you another good place," added Sofiya. "Follow me."

They did.

4

EMMA URGED ON THE TREMBLING TEMPLAR AS THEY passed a maze of rooms, each crowded with three or four sleeping men, women, and children. The diverse ages and genders huddled together under blankets, taking full advantage of their combined body heat.

Led by Sofiya, Emma and Templar sidestepped the sleeping forms and continued on to what appeared to be a dead end.

"Where are we?" Emma asked. She was trying to visualize where they were relative to the rest of the building.

The teen pointed back from where they came.

"Kitchen that way."

She then pointed to a narrow hallway entrance on the other side of the room.

"That leads to stairs—not the big stairs from the lobby, but short stairs from here to roof."

Sofiya then moved away an old highboy and slid open a false wall. Behind it was a cramped but clean cubicle.

"You can hide here," she said. "Built during Stalin Terror. They say five scientists hid for six months."

Emma thought of Anne Frank hiding from the Nazis. When she heard the squawk of walkie-talkies, she remembered Anne died in captivity.

Sofiya heard it, also, raced to the closest window, pulled back a tattered bit of sheeting, and nervously glanced outside.

The original Range Rover had multiplied to a fleet. Jeeps and other 4X4s formed a heavy-treaded fist around the building.

Ilya was in the street, flanked by footsoldiers, barking orders at Igor.

"Seal every exit. If they're still in there, there'll be no way out. We'll search every apartment!"

He turned abruptly, snapped his fingers, and a cadre of uniformed militia followed him into the building.

Sofiya hurried the wet Templar and the dry-mouthed Emma inside the cubicle.

"They can search all they want," insisted Sofiya, "they will never find you. You very safe."

"What about you?" asked Emma.

"I take care of me, you hide."

Sofiya replaced the false wall and the highboy, and the two sequestered fugitives heard her footsteps as she left the room.

The cramped space was spottily illumined by thin light shafts entering through tiny breathing holes. Emma felt like a boxed hamster.

She looked at the drained and pasty face of the man she knew as Thomas More. She knew his name wasn't

Thomas More. She also knew she was going to undress him.

"This isn't quite the way I imagined this happening," admitted Emma with feigned joviality, "but I have to take your clothes off and get you warm before your body shuts down. You have hypothermia, my drowned poet . . . or drowned rat."

She tugged, pulled, unbuttoned, unzipped, and removed every soaked item of clothing clinging to Templar's pale frame. She towel dried him, and held him close to her own warmth.

"Do you feel anything? Talk to me, tell me you feel warm."

To Simon Templar, the tiny pinpoints of light seemed to sparkle and dance like bright stars in a clear night sky—a night sky in another time, another land, another life.

"Agnes, my love . . ."

Emma's eyebrows arched in the dark.

"Your kiss, Agnes . . ."

Whoever this Agnes was, she must be one hot number.

Emma sighed.

There's nothing like hypothermia-induced delirium to bring out the naked truth, she thought.

And then she saw something that took her breath away.

His eyes brimmed with tears.

She held him tight, then tighter, rocking him as a mother would a feverish child.

"Tell me," her voice was soft as cotton, "tell me all about it. . . ."

And he did.

Cradled in her arms, it was as if he were a child of

tender years nourished from the breast of mercy. He spoke to her warmth, and if the narrative lacked elements of cohesion, it was unmistakably authentic.

It was all there—St. Ignatius, the boys and girls, nuns and priests, dogs, danger, and death in the moonlight. The long-withheld tears broke through the mesh of cold emotion and poured as a torrent down the mountainside of his cheeks.

He did not sob, nor did he cry. It was rather as if the sadness and pain of a quarter century had risen to the surface of his life and, having reached the deep blue pools of his eyes, overflowed for once and forever.

Emma held him closer, kissing the corners of his beautiful eyes.

"I've never felt quite like this before," admitted Templar.

"What do you mean?" asked Emma hopefully.

"I'm freezing, what do you think I mean?"

She giggled, and the fact that she giggled in this most repressive and traumatic of environments, and under such life-threatening conditions, amused them both.

Emma knew she couldn't allow Templar to lose consciousness. She had to keep him alert and conversational.

"What's your name? Who are you, really?"

"My name is Simon, Simon Templar. . . ." His answer was almost unconvincing.

"So, were you really named for a saint?"

He laughed a wet but honest laugh.

"No, I was named after a character in a paperback book—Knight Templar."

"The hero of a thousand adventures?" Emma knew the book, the character.

Templar's eyes brightened.

"You've heard of *Knight Templar*?"

She smiled. "Sure. My father had tons of that sort of stuff," replied Emma, doing her best to sound nonchalant. "If you would've spent more time in my apartment, you would have found an entire cardboard box filled with back issues of *Thriller—The Paper of a Thousand Thrills.*"

"You're the woman of my dreams." He said it as if it were a joke, but he meant it.

"In case you haven't noticed," said Emma, "I'm not quite as buxom as the women on the covers of those old blood-and-thunder adventures."

Templar eyed her bosom as best he could.

"Yeah, but you've had things in your brassiere they could never dream of."

She kissed him, held him to her as if they were one, and they both became conscious of his nakedness.

"There's nothing wrong with you now, that's for sure. As long as you're up," quipped Emma, "you might as well get dressed."

She handed him the oddball selection of Russian fashion from the kitchen clothesline and pressed her ear against the false wall to listen for sounds of danger. She heard nothing.

"Maybe we won't be in here long," she said hopefully. "Sofiya said we were safe. If the coast is clear . . ."

The coast was far from clear.

Ilya and his men worked their way through the building, sniffing out the trail of the teenage trollop named Sofiya. The welcome afforded him by the lower floors' residents was cold and unconcerned. They suggested he try one floor up.

He did. And the next floor above that as well. Each successive floor held more people, and more contradictory advice as to Sofiya's whereabouts.

Between the fifth and sixth floor, Ilya made an astonishing discovery—a small puddle of water similar to other puddles of water he'd encountered on the stairs. Without giving it serious consideration, he assumed the roof leaked.

He now gave it serious consideration, and a sly grin crept across his face.

"Oh, we've got you now," he said, and they followed the wet trail to the ninth floor. Within minutes Ilya was holding court in the communal apartment's crowded kitchen. In one hand was his Smith & Wesson, in the other, a large wad of American bills.

"Five hundred bucks reward, all in American currency, to whoever hands over the two foreigners. I don't care about the little slut who brought 'em here," declared Ilya offensively, "I just want the damn foreigners."

He turned to the potbellied man who held a mop in one hand and his bottle of kvass in the other.

"How 'bout you, Tubby, seen any Americans or Brits?"

"No, but I did see one polar bear. Do I get two-fifty?"

The foot soldiers snickered.

Ilya smiled. Then he calmly shot the old man through the heart. The foot soldiers stopped snickering. Sofiya's mother sobbed uncontrollably.

The gunshot echoed through the ninth floor, awaking the huddled residents and penetrating the false wall. Emma and Templar pulled each other tight in silence.

Ilya crossed over to the old woman, took her hand, and kissed it. She looked as if she wanted to vomit. She abruptly turned and ran out of the room.

"Was it something I said?" called out Ilya mockingly.

Templar and Emma pressed their ears against the wall. They heard one person's rapidly approaching footsteps.

"Maybe it's Sofiya," whispered Emma hopefully.

"Don't count on it," said Templar. He stood with determination, bracing himself for whatever came next.

"Here! Here! The foreigners are here! Help! Help!"

It was the old crone turned traitor, cawing out a summons to Ilya and his militia. Her nostrils flared and her lips twitched as she cried out.

For an instant Templar and Emma were too stupefied to move. Then, as if launched by a rocket, the Saint threw himself against the false wall. The plaster smashed to a thousand dusty pieces; the highboy slammed against the floor. The woman screamed and flailed her arms like a human pinwheel.

They were out.

Templar and Emma raced down the narrow corridor toward the short flight to the roof.

"The stairs! The stairs!" screeched the old woman.

Ilya and his men crashed out of the kitchen, and Vlad momentarily became entangled in the makeshift clothesline.

"C'mon, dammit!" barked Ilya. He stumbled through the apartment to the only stairs he knew—the winding concrete stairwell reaching from lobby to rooftop.

Templar and Emma quickly ascended the narrow

wooden stairs. At the top of the short flight was a trapdoor. Emma pushed it, but its ice-encrusted frame wouldn't budge.

"No!" she cried out in anguish. She was becoming desperate.

Templar added his muscle to her efforts, and the ice around the wooden trap broke free with a loud snap. He pushed Emma out ahead of him onto the broad, flat rooftop and scrambled after her.

They desperately scanned the wind-whipped roof, seeking an avenue of escape.

"Can we jump to the next building?" Emma asked, astonished that she would even think of doing it.

There was a building within jumping distance, but the roof was a sheet of ice beneath their feet.

Templar's mind raced; his eyes seeking another solution. "There!"

"Where?"

Templar grabbed her under the elbow and yanked her toward a sheet-metal utility shed in the middle of the roof. A swift kick to the door shattered away all ice around the frame and gave them entry.

"We can't hide in there," objected Emma incredulously.

"Who's hiding?" Templar pulled her inside. "We're leaving!"

He pushed past random tools and tar paper to the cluster of utility pipes arising from a wide shaft.

"Oh, God," exclaimed Emma, "you're not thinking of . . ."

He was.

When Ilya and his cadre of thugs charged up the concrete stairwell and banged out through the metal fire door onto the roof, he should have expected what he saw. Nothing. Again. Almost nothing—a utility shed with ice broken around the doorframe.

"There!" yelled Ilya, slapping Igor on the arm and pointing. "The shed!"

Igor impulsively pumped several shells into either side before kicking open the door. Vlad, his shoes devoid of his compatriots' off-road tread, slid stupidly around in a circle before falling on his rear.

Templar and Emma had not cowered in the shed awaiting inevitable perforation. They had wrapped their coats around the utility pipes and slid down the hundred-foot shaft.

Had it been a carnival ride, Emma might have enjoyed it. Probably not; she was not the carnival type. Fearing for her life every inch of the speedy, perilous descent, she was too terrified to scream.

Igor, better intentioned than bred, sprayed a deafening hail of hot lead down the shaft just as Emma and Simon touched bottom and exploded out into the basement.

Fuming with anger and frustration, Ilya whacked the automatic off target. Then he whacked Igor.

"We want her alive! Him you can kill; her you can wound. But don't kill her! Idyot!"

Ten floors below, Emma, overwhelmed, leaned against the dark basement's empty oil tank. She gulped air and popped a heart pill. "I can't believe I did that," she gasped.

Templar, finding the adrenaline rush curative, had already found the light switch. A yellow bulb on a long cord dangled above them, providing minimal illumination.

"No time to relax now," he said seriously. "The

American Embassy is east of here. They can't touch us there."

"East? How can you tell which way is east?"

He held up his penknife. "There's a compass built in."

"Do you have a blowtorch in that thing, too?"

"I've told you too many secrets already," said the Saint, and he began searching the basement for direct access to Moscow's extensive underground.

The American Embassy's location was no secret, and Ilya could see the Stars and Stripes proudly waving from his position on the rooftop.

"Damn! They'll be heading for the embassy! Let's go!"

Heading for the embassy, indeed, but not by the most direct route. Instead of emerging at street level and attempting to outrun and outwit Tretiak's team, Templar sought out the dank basement's sewer outlet and service tunnel—primary indicators of access to the underground world of black market deal making, clandestine retail outlets, and dissident hideouts.

Having discovered the opening, he yanked out the metal grate and pulled Emma after him into the maze of subterranean Moscow.

Cringing from the dirt, darkness, and disorientation, Emma demanded to know where they were.

"We are under the street, under the buildings," explained Templar. "This isn't unusual, it's simply that most people never think about the city under the city."

"I don't," confirmed Emma without the slightest trace of humor.

Templar glanced again at his compass, then led his wary companion around another dark corner.

"Most major cities, especially old ones—even American ones like New York and Seattle—have an entire subterranean culture," he continued. "It used to be that the lower-class workers couldn't be seen above ground except on the job."

Emma was not interested in social history. "Are we there yet? I see lights."

She also heard voices. One of them was decidedly female.

Templar stopped when he saw an attractive woman in her mid-twenties coming toward them, gesturing wildly.

"Hurry, in here! You're the Americans?!"

5

EMMA LOOKED AT TEMPLAR; TEMPLAR LOOKED AT Emma. They both looked at the slender, curly-haired woman who seemed overly enthusiastic to see them.

"Expecting us?" asked Templar.

The girl laughed and motioned for them to follow her.

Emma wished she were home with her fish.

Dark, cramped, and as dismal as an air-raid shelter was the subterranean depot into which they were summoned. But propped against the dirt walls, lit by oil lamps, were gilt-edged embroidery. The room was filled with silver chalices and various authentic or replicated Russian Orthodox sacramental objects.

In the corner a nerdy young man was polishing a pendant.

"That's Toli, my curator, and I'm Alexa Frankievitch, but since you're Americans, you can call me Frankie."

"How did you know . . . ?"

"Oh, I've been expecting a happy American couple looking for valuable religious relics. In fact, I was expecting you an hour ago. I thought you got lost."

Frankie turned to her vast display of items for sale.

"I can sell you all manner of religious relics and semiauthentic antiques," she insisted.

Templar leaned over and whispered in Emma's ear.

"She thinks we're somebody else."

"No kidding," hissed Emma. "Let's get going."

When Frankie turned back around, Simon attempted to confront the situation directly.

"Frankie, listen, all we want is—"

"I know, I know," interrupted the energetic young woman, "the icon of the Virgin of the Don. I need thirty-thousand dollars American up-front."

"No, no . . ." Emma tried to intercede and explain.

"Okay, twenty thousand, not a penny less," Frankie relented, unaware that no one was bargaining with her. "C'mon. It's the very icon Prince Donskoy carried into battle against the Tatars, who retreated, was a miracle—"

"I don't believe in miracles," Templar cut in brusquely. He picked up a jewel encrusted chalice and spun it in the air. "Whadya do, Frankie, stamp these replicas out by the dozens?"

Frankie stomped a small boot and shook her curly hair in agitation and mock anger.

"That's authentic. Everything here is authentic."

Simon set the glass decorated chalice down as if it were valuable and grabbed Emma by the hand. "Let's go."

Frankie swiftly interposed herself in the doorway.

"Five thousand for the icon. Final offer. Not including cost to smuggle it through tunnels out of town."

Templar's eyes lit up when he realized she was gesturing at maps which detailed Moscow's extensive underground.

He was about to speak when they heard the pounding of boots in the distance.

"Bastards!" hissed Frankie. "You've brought the police!"

"No, they're not police," countered Templar emphatically. "They're 'comrade criminals'—Tretiak's goon squad."

Frankie's eyes widened at the sound of Tretiak's name. She unleashed a stream of Russian expletives and grabbed an oil lamp off the wall as Toli extinguished the rest. Frankie then gestured Templar and Emma back into the labyrinth, and Toli expertly sealed up the relic-packed depot.

"Please help us," entreated Emma. "We're just trying to get to the American Embassy."

They all saw the faint glow of approaching firelight. They didn't need to know exactly who was coming— the phrase *Tretiak's goons* said it all.

It was Vlad, sans teeth, and several Tretiak Security stalking through the maze, armed with torches and guns like a lynch mob.

If Frankie and Toli consulted on an agreed course of action, they did it telepathically.

"Follow me," ordered Frankie. "We'll have to go the long way, but we won't let them get you. There is exit hatch just under Embassy bomb shelter."

The Saint was skeptical; Emma was impressed.

"How do you know the underground of Moscow so well?"

"We *are* the underground of Moscow," answered Frankie dryly.

It seemed like hours, and perhaps it was, as the tired and filthy foursome stumbled around another bend. Frankie, much to Templar's consternation, seemed to be having trouble getting her bearings.

"Are we lost?"

"You're in Russia, sir," explained the gregarious Frankie. "Its tunnels are mysterious and illogical as . . . well . . . the Motherland herself!"

Templar's eyes narrowed. "But you *do* know the way. . . ."

"Of course," insisted Frankie, "like I know the face of a stainless-steel Bulgari Chronograph."

She was staring at Templar's five-thousand dollar wristwatch.

He pulled it off with a faint growl and handed it over.

Frankie, infatuated with her new timepiece, had a sudden refreshment of memory. "This way!"

Hunched low, Templar and Emma followed Frankie and Toli to a walkway leading to a compression hatchwheel.

"The water main," explained their energetic guide, "because of rationing, they shut it down each afternoon."

"And they turn it back on . . . ?" asked Templar.

Frankie checked her new Chronograph.

"Hmmm, 'bout five minutes, plus or minus."

No time to lose.

Templar was already at the hatch, melting the rusted lock mechanism with a tiny-but-mighty blowtorch attachment to his penknife. Emma, surprised by technological breakthrough, shook her head.

"That damn thing *does* have a blowtorch!"

Frankie offered Simon a few nuggets of further guidance.

"The third hatchwheel is under your embassy. Make it to number three and you're home free."

She gave poor distraught Emma a good-luck embrace. Then, seized with transports of conscience, she took off Templar's watch and handed it to Emma.

"Here. Take it. Honest. I've got one just like it at home."

Frankie and Toli hurried off as the hatchwheel opened. Templar climbed in and extended a hand to Emma.

The tunnels of Moscow's underground labyrinth were as fun as Chutes & Ladders compared to the pitch-black metallic universe of the large pipe in which Emma and Templar now found themselves.

The Saint pulled out his penknife—the one that had been a blowtorch only moments before—and stuck it between his teeth. A powerful high-intensity bulb burned at its tip, shining a shaft of light ahead of them.

"I'm an idiot, Simon," noted Dr. Emma Russell. "I'm wasting my time with cold fusion."

"Huh?" Templar couldn't articulate too well with a light in his teeth.

"I should market that penknife of yours and retire."

At least Emma was loosening up.

"I hate to think what you do with that thing when you're alone," she muttered.

The two fugitives crawled as quickly as they could along the cold pathway of pipe. Progress was tedious but constant.

Templar shone his penknife light at an exit hatch above them.

" 'Hatch Number Two,' " he read the attached tag.

"Novinsky Street. I figure we have two more minutes, unless our plus is a minus."

Plus or minus. Emma shuddered at the implications.

Soon his penlight found the embassy exit hatch. No hatchwheel; no exit.

"Oh, my God . . ." Emma gasped. "We've got to go all the way back! We've been three minutes, ten seconds . . ."

Templar gaped at the sight of his watch.

"You stole that back from her?"

"No. *I'm* not a thief," snapped Emma testily. "She returned it."

Templar, astounded, grabbed the watch back and strapped it on.

"Crawl backward," he commanded, "till we get to that second hatch. Hurry!"

In the distance the sound of whooshing water signaled the oncoming rush of wet death.

They scurried for their lives, scraping their hands and knees on the pipe's rough metal. Soon they reached the Novinsky Street hatch. Simon attempted spinning the hatchwheel. It wouldn't budge.

The whooshing increased in volume, and the pipe began to vibrate. Simon put his ear to the hatchwheel.

"What are you doing?" demanded Emma.

"Pretending I'm George Sanders," he murmured.

He listened, he felt, he hauled off and whacked the hatchwheel as hard as he could. It spun beneath his grip.

The hatch opened and he pulled himself up into the service vent, then he reached down for Emma. She grasped his strong grip and he yanked her up just as water roared through the pipe below. It geysered through the hatch, soaking them both.

Templar slammed the hatch shut, but the pressure was too intense. The water erupted into the vent, rising rapidly to waist level.

"Help me!" he shouted. "Stand on it!"

Emma added her efforts to his, forcing the hatch against the mounting pressure. It closed, and he spun the wheel shut.

They stood there, stressed but safe, wet and momentarily silent.

At length, perhaps it was a few seconds, Emma spoke.

"I'd have heart failure, but it would take too much effort."

Templar kissed her cheek impulsively, gestured for her to stay put, and clambered up the ladder to the manhole lid.

He popped his head up, and out of the darkness came the headlights of Ilya's Range Rover searing straight toward him. He ducked back down as the 4X4 parked directly over the manhole cover.

The Saint, flashing an optimistic grin, scurried down the ladder.

"Uh-oh," remarked Emma. "When a man smiles in a sewer, I get worried."

"They're right above us," announced Templar pleasantly.

Emma coughed out a jittery laugh.

Templar began tapping a pipe running through the service vent.

"You know why it's not cold in the American Embassy?" he asked.

She looked at the pipe and understood. It was a gas line. A gas line into which Simon Templar was plunging the blade of his versatile penknife. When he pulled it free, she heard the distinctive hiss of escaping gas.

Emma blinked in disbelief.

"For a suicide pact, you need my permission." Her voice trembled.

"Not suicide," explained Simon, "survival."

He started up the ladder, motioning her to follow. She balked.

"Would you rather suffocate?"

It was an easy decision. In the next second they were both hurrying up the ladder. He lifted the manhole cover again, and they slithered out under Ilya's vehicle.

They lay there gulping fresh air, as a pair of black paraboots jumped down to the pavement. Soon several pair of loafers and Nikes appeared.

The American Embassy was one hundred yards away, and with the foot soldiers right above them, it felt like a hundred miles.

Emma was in despair; the Saint was in control.

"Trust me on this," he whispered. "They'll open the gate when they see you coming."

"They'll open fire when they see *you* coming," said Emma, referring to Ilya and the thugs.

"It will take less than ten seconds for you to get to safety," insisted Templar.

"Me? What about you?" Emma was starting to panic. She popped another little pill.

"Consider me one of life's little distractions," he said, and before she could protest, he rolled out from under the vehicle. Simon sprang to his feet and strolled pleasantly past Ilya as if trying to brazen his way to freedom.

Stunned by this gambit, Ilya yelped like a wounded Pomeranian. Vlad and Igor jumped for Templar, and he allowed them to take him down.

Emma realized that she would never have a better moment to break cover, took a breath, and ran like hell for the embassy gates.

Ilya immediately realized what was happening and took off furiously after her.

The on-duty Marines behind the embassy gate helplessly watched as Ilya gained on Emma.

"American!" yelled Emma. "Open up!"

She was almost at the gate; Ilya was almost at her back.

The Marines did all they were allowed to do. They swung open the gate.

Emma's legs pumped furiously as she ran fast, then faster, but Ilya's outstretched arm was on her. He clutched her coat, pulling her back.

And Emma threw herself forward, arms back like an Olympic diver, and the coat peeled off in his grasp. She passed through the gate as if it were the finish line, triumphantly ringed by Marines.

"I'm an American citizen," panted Emma breathlessly.

The Marines assured her of full protection and threw malevolent glares at Ilya.

"Back off from the gate—now!"

Ilya obeyed, but his eyes bored holes through the Marines' uniform.

Emma had escaped, but Ilya had a consolation prize—the Saint.

Igor and Vlad held the battered, bruised, but exultant captive. Templar was about to prick Ilya with a witty insult, but a quick gun butt to the head canceled the remark and sent him sprawling to the pavement.

The trip was worth the pain—from this vantage point he could see the escaping gas cause visible ripples in the air as it billowed out of the open manhole beneath the Range Rover.

Ilya straddled him triumphantly. Concealing his gun with the flap of his open coat, he pressed the barrel to Templar's temple and leaned down into his face.

"One shot left," stated Ilya, his foul breath stinging Simon's nostrils. "You can't come all the way to Russia and not play Russian roulette."

Templar felt the cold steel pressing against his head as he looked Ilya in the eye. Without knowing how quick the other was on the trigger, he estimated that he had a sporting chance of knocking the gun aside and landing an iron fist where it would obliterate Ilya's nose. But there were still the other men to reckon with.

That moment's swift and instinctive reckoning of his chances was probably what helped to save him. And in that time he also forced himself to realize that the fleeting pleasure of pushing Ilya's front teeth through the back of his neck would ring down the curtain on his only hope of getaway. Besides, he had already initiated his preferred plan of escape. All he needed was a little more time.

Emma, safe but helpless behind the embassy gate, watched through a veil of tears.

As Ilya spun the cylinder, Templar's hand moved slowly toward his bootheel.

"Before you shoot me, don't you want to know where all the money is hidden?"

Ilya's finger was already exerting pressure on the trigger. As Templar removed the penknife from his heel, the cylinder rolled and the hammer came down.

Click!

Empty chamber.

Ilya spun it again. There was no bullet visible. This was it.

"What money?" Ilya asked.

"Tretiak's. Daddy's. Your father's got billions stashed and I know where it is," lied Templar. "Let's make a deal."

Ilya didn't trust him. They locked eyes, and Templar triggered the tiny hidden blowtorch into operation.

"Here's your deal. . . ." said Ilya with a sick sneer. He pressed the barrel tighter against Templar's head.

Templar flicked the blowtorch under the Range Rover, and Ilya saw him do it. Before he could process the implications or pull the trigger, his world violently erupted in a searing fireball of flame.

The Range Rover was airborne in one direction, Ilya was thrown in the other, and Simon Templar was on his feet.

The Saint threw Emma one last look through the inferno and vanished behind the billowing smoke and crashing, incinerated auto parts.

6

THE WARMTH AND SECURITY OF THE AMERICAN EM-
bassy was, after the series of life-threatening episodes,
a haven of rest for Dr. Emma Russell.

Cleaned up and changed into loaned clothes a size
too big, she was soon politely escorted through formal-
ities by a few good Marines.

"You just have to fill out a form before we put you
on a flight home," explained her courteous, uniformed
attendant as they passed the impressive embassy seal,
flanked by flags. "Any medical conditions, that sort
of thing."

"Actually, my heart, I . . ." Emma paused and
smiled at a sudden realization. "I haven't taken a pill
in hours. I ran for my life and my heart wasn't pounding. You'd think I would have dropped dead before I
got to the gate."

"Sometimes our bodies surprise us," agreed the

Marine. "We often underestimate our own survival skills."

"No kidding," Emma said with a laugh, "if you would have told me two days ago what I was going to go through, I never would have believed it."

Her escort gestured at a processing center at the end of the corridor. It was crowded with other Americans also eager to leave Moscow's mounting social turbulence.

"Get your form at window five," he advised. "We'll be back for you at nineteen-hundred hours—a full Marine escort to the airport."

Before Emma could thank them, the two Marines crisply peeled off to the right. She continued toward processing, past numerous embassy officials aiding other travelers. As she approached window five, an affable bearded official came up beside her. He spoke in a strong Southern accent.

"Straubing."

"I beg your pardon?" Emma didn't understand.

He smiled and held out his hand. "Straubing."

"What's a straubing?"

"I am. That's my name. Harold Straubing."

Emma, embarrassed, blushed and felt foolish. "I'm sorry, Mr. Straubing, I'm a bit flustered. I've been through a lot in the last few days."

"So, where does a nice little lady like you think she's going?"

"Back to London . . ."

Straubing gently clasped his hand above her elbow and guided her away from window five.

"I don't think that's a wise idea," he said, and his accent disappeared. She recognized the voice, and blinked at him in disbelief.

"Simon! Are you crazy? I'm safe. I'm on the next flight. . . ."

Templar stopped in front of a heavily barred window. "Look out there."

Through the bars, Emma saw a gaggle of demonstrators on the plaza. Among them were Ilya's goons, Vlad and Igor, patiently waiting.

"If you make it to the airport, they'll get you on the plane," stated Simon flatly, and Emma shuddered.

"What do I do?" Her voice trembled. Her feelings of safety and security were quickly evaporating.

"As long as you're here, you're safe. Tell the Marines you've developed a sudden fear of flying—post traumatic stress and all that. They'll believe you, you're a doctor. Then find a computer and a quiet room, finish the formula, and fax it to me."

"Just like that?" Emma was incredulous. "Finish the formula and fax it to you?"

He handed her a number.

"This is your Moscow office?" Her tone was tinged with sarcasm.

"Portable fax, one international number that works anywhere," responded the Saint cheerfully. "Modern technology at its most compassionate."

She peered hard at his face.

"Speaking of compassion, are you sure this is about my safety and not your retirement fund? How do I know you're not going to sell the formula—again?"

"Again, you'll have to trust me."

He resumed striding, and she walked at his side as if he were giving her an official tour.

"Of course I trust you, Mr. Straubing. I mean Mr. More, uh, Mr. Farrar, I mean Mr. de Porres . . . after all, you're my personal saint."

Simon smiled.

"To be a saint, you've got to be linked to three miracles. Don't ruin my reputation, Emma."

With that, he turned off down a hallway and blended in with busy embassy bureaucrats. She watched him go, still wondering if he were truly trustworthy or if she was about to be burned.

The burns inflicted upon Ilya in the Range Rover explosion were, according to his doctor, healing nicely with no sign of infection.

Ilya allowed a nurse to apply salve to his blisters while the house-call physician completed his follow-up exam. The doctor was more concerned with the decor of Ilya's room—swastikas and Nazi flags—than he was with the thug's injuries.

Tretiak, impatient and fed up with his son's self-centered whining, paced nervously around the room.

"All in all," remarked the doctor, "I'd say your son is a lucky boy."

"Lucky? Look at me," objected Ilya, "my cheek is singed! I look like a refugee from hell!"

"No, I mean you're lucky because hundreds of thousands of Russians gave their lives to defeat the Nazis in World War II," blurted out the angry physician. "You're lucky some patriot hasn't killed you for being a goddam Nazi yourself."

Ilya brayed like an ass. "That stupid war was over years before I was born, Doc. Nobody remembers and nobody cares."

The doctor remembered; the doctor cared.

Ilya's exasperated father stalked from the room and almost collided with Botvin, who had been nervously awaiting an audience.

"I've run every test on Russell's cold fusion formula," stammered the little scientist, "and I've concluded that her formula is not incomplete—it's impossible!"

This was not a good time to bring discouraging words. Tretiak erupted with almost as much incendiary power as Ilya's 4X4.

"I invest millions and you can't make it work?"

Botvin had a sudden mental image of imminent death.

"But I've been working on it without sleep for nearly two weeks," stammered Botvin, backtracking to a positive perspective. "At first blush the theorem appears quite impressive. . . ."

Tretiak stopped midstride and turned slowly to face Botvin. The scientist took two wary steps back and held his breath. The face of Ivan Tretiak was no longer distorted by anger; rather, it was wreathed in what could be mistaken for a warm smile.

"You did just say 'quite impressive,' didn't you?"

Botvin rattled his head up and down.

"Good! Stay impressed! Good man! We can use it to destroy our enemies."

Tretiak strode to the banister and bellowed down to the foyer, summoning his chief operating officer.

"Vereshagin, arrange a meeting!"

"With whom, Mr. Tretiak?"

"The President of Russia! I want Botvin and me to see him tomorrow night at the Kremlin!"

Botvin blinked rapidly and moved closer to ask a question of penultimate importance.

"Me? Meet with the President? But why?"

Tretiak threw a large arm around the small man's shoulders. "As the capitalists say: You don't sell the steak, you sell the sizzle. We're going to sell Karpov ten billion dollars' worth of sizzle."

Vereshagin called the Kremlin, carefully wording Tretiak's demand as a polite, respectful request. The message's essence was immediately relayed to Nikolai Korshunov, the president's chief of staff, who delivered it personally to his superior.

President Karpov was well aware of two dreadful facts of life: (1) Ivan Tretiak was his most volatile and powerful opponent, and (2) Ivan Tretiak was undoubtedly behind the inexplicable energy crisis.

If Tretiak wanted to meet with him, Karpov would be a fool to resist and a fool to comply. He chose the lesser foolishness and scheduled the meeting.

The following evening Ivan Tretiak, trailed by Vereshagin, Ilya, and Botvin, was escorted through the Kremlin's impressive corridors by uniformed guards. He stopped to admire and covet the ceremonial sabers, Fabergé eggs, and priceless tapestries. The guards, well aware of their guest's identity and reputation, regarded Tretiak and his associates with deserved suspicion.

Botvin, perspiring terribly, girded himself for the upcoming deception while father and son conferred.

"Only that scientist can spoil my plan," Tretiak whispered urgently to Ilya, "if she gets back to London and talks to the press . . ."

"Don't worry," Ilya replied smugly. "Dr. Russell's plane won't leave the runway—at least not in one piece."

The three charlatans were officiously directed into a heavily secured Kremlin meeting room. Awaiting them at an impressive hardwood conference table were a wary and careworn President Karpov and Nikolai Korshunov.

"Welcome, gentlemen," said Karpov coolly, and he motioned for them to sit opposite him.

Tretiak and Botvin sat, but Ilya lingered at the door like a sulking guard dog.

Ivan Tretiak shivered with theatrical gusto. "Chilly in here, Mr. President."

"As long as the heating crisis persists, we keep our thermostat quite low." The president spoke with presidential politeness.

"Yes, let us discuss the heating crisis, Mr. President," Tretiak leaned forward, fixing his gaze on Karpov. "As former minister of energy and power, I hear all manner of schemes to provide cheaper power. . . ."

"I'm sure you have," offered Karpov with a hint of cynicism.

Tretiak continued as if the remark had not been made.

"Our countrymen are freezing to death, Mr. President, but I have become aware of a marvelous new technology about which I am hopelessly out of my league from a scientific viewpoint. That's why I've brought our eminent physicist here, Lev Botvin, from the University of Moscow."

Documents, charts, graphs, and assorted impressive pieces of paper were shuffled and handed, as a matter of protocol, to Korshunov.

He began flipping through the pages while Karpov looked on.

"Before we're dazzled by the good news," offered Korshunov, "let's dispense with the bad. What's the price of this 'marvel'?"

Vereshagin leaned across the table, finding the relevant page.

"Here. Right here are the research and development costs. Those are the only costs—I repeat—the only costs you're asked to defray."

Karpov leaned over and cast an interested glance at the figures. When he saw the total, he almost fell off his presidential chair.

"Ten billion?! My God! You must be mad!"

Tretiak started to rise. Vereshagin and Botvin followed his lead.

Karpov motioned them back down.

"Wait, wait," he said with forced joviality, "I thought we'd drink some Kremlyovakaya to get a bit warmer and discuss all this in more detail."

Tretiak smiled.

Korshunov arose from the table and moved to a bookcase shelf. Hidden behind was a crystal decanter of vodka and some tumblers.

"Mr. President," began Tretiak as he sat back down, "in all candor, I'm tired of these silly partisan political struggles. You ask the average Russian and he or she will tell you that politicians are boring, fighting is a waste of time, and that what we need is more comfort and less speeches."

Karpov nodded. He wanted to know where Tretiak was going with this.

"If a major scientific breakthrough such as the one we are asking you to fund would bring warmth and happiness to the people, I would gladly devote my time and my life to my family business and . . . my dear family." He threw an almost believable sentimental look at Ilya.

Karpov wasn't gullible. He knew Tretiak was as sentimental as a rabid Doberman.

"In other words," clarified the president, "you would withdraw your opposition?"

Tretiak showed his teeth in an approximation of a sincere smile. "It is my sweetest dream."

The message was clear. Karpov looked at Korshunov. The latter poured the vodka.

"Without making any sort of commitment," said Karpov officiously, "we wish to study these documents. Dr. Botvin, will you kindly explain, in layman's terms, this cold fusion?"

Botvin cleared his throat, repositioned his fogged lenses, and began his elaborate, yet simple, explanation—an explanation not intended to make cold fusion any more understandable, but to make the ten billion in hard currency more obtainable.

He was, in effect, drawing a verbal map from Karpov's wallet to Tretiak's pocket.

PART THREE

1

"As the number of deaths from freezing mounts, the mood here is increasingly ominous," stated CNN correspondent Jan Sharp broadcasting from an improvised canopy outside the Kremlin. "A bankrupt Russian government—unable to provide the heating oil its people so desperately need—claims to be working on some mysterious solution to the crisis."

The street was strewn with broken bottles, charred trashcans, torn clothes, spent teargas cartridges, and Tretiak placards.

"Meanwhile," continued Sharp, "what Ivan Tretiak's Oktober Party bills as rallies are turning into nightly riots. . . ."

Detailing the debris and disorder prevalent in Moscow, the newscaster paid no notice to the rain-slickered businessman edging past the clutter, folding his umbrella, and entering a small side-street shop.

Dark and narrow, the counters were crammed with cheap copies of Russian Orthodox art, cardboard icons, plastic chalices, tin pendants, and other low-rent replicas similar to the more authentic-looking items Templar had seen in the Moscow underground.

The owner, wearing an overcoat indoors and pacing the small space to stay warm, was the same woman who dealt in higher-priced but equally bogus items below ground.

"Excuse me," said the businessman with a New Orleans accent, "but I'm looking for either an authentic relic from the estate of the late Prince von Oldenburg who was married to a sister of the czar, or a genuine Madonna icon. . . ."

Frankie brightened, sensing a score.

"With an American dollar deposit, we could meet somewhere else. I can show you rare objects. Prince von Oldenburg"—she gave the name serious thought—"very rare, very famous. His grandson was a movie star, did you know that? See him on pirate videotapes from America. Old black and white." Frankie made a motion with her hands as if turning a combination lock. "Breaking open the bad guy's safe; breaking the women's hearts, yes? A true Russian!"

She laughed, crinkling her eyes in a devilish smile.

"We'll see what we can find from royalty formerly known as Prince. As for Madonna, Madonna costs a bit extra—"

"That's fine," he replied seriously. "But she's gotta be wearing the cone-shaped bra."

Frankie blinked in disbelief, then took a good look at the customer.

"Hey. Mr. Bulgari Chronograph. Real funny. Didn't you make it out?"

"Almost, but I decided to stay."

She squinted suspiciously. "Then, why're you back, Bulgari?"

It was time for some truth telling. "My name is Templar, Simon Templar."

He put out his hand in friendship, but Frankie didn't take it. She glanced dubiously from his hand to his face.

"The men looking for you were crawling all over the tunnels like rats. They roughed me up, but I laughed in their faces. I said I didn't know anything. . . ."

Templar started to smile in appreciation, but it was cut short by her next remark.

". . . so they shot Toli."

Simon put his hand down. "I'm sorry, really. In a way, it's partially my fault. . . ."

"No, Tretiak's fault," insisted Frankie. "They would have killed you and your girlfriend, too. Where is she?"

"The American Embassy. She's safe, for now, but this entire country is in danger."

Frankie forced a rueful laugh. "No surprise. No justice."

" 'The best beloved of all things in my sight is justice,' " said Templar, and he meant it.

"Wrong time, wrong town."

Templar took a breath.

"I need your help to stop Tretiak."

She stepped back defensively.

"Hey, it's a big country—big country—and you're saying I'm your best friend here?"

"I'm saying you're my *only* friend."

She looked away, pretending to examine a cardboard replica of the Kremlin. She was, in reality, reexamining her own personal commitment to an ethical standard above and beyond the selfishness, corruption, and materialism devouring her homeland.

"Sometimes a person has to look the other way," she said softly, "and other times a person can't look away at all."

She turned back toward him, shrugged as if her important thoughts were of little consequence, and smiled.

"Just don't get me killed, okay?"

They shook hands.

Frankie then offered him bitter instant coffee in a plastic cup, locked the front door, and put the CLOSED sign in the window.

"What happens now?" she asked, rubbing her hands together in conspiratorial glee.

A light seemed to glow in Templar's sapphire eyes.

"We light a fire under Ivan Tretiak."

"Hoo-boy! I can picture that." Frankie liked the plan so far.

"We're going to get a rise out of that would-be tin-pot dictator, Frankie. In fact, believe that he'll rise like a loaf overloaded with young and vigorous yeast."

She found his delivery amusing, his material adequate.

"When he's finished rising," elaborated Templar, "he'll have such an altitude that he'll have to climb a ladder to take off his shoes."

Frankie laughed for the first time since Toli's death, and color came into her cheeks. "Very funny picture in my head about that!"

"Frankie," said Templar as he toyed with a Kremlin replica, "there are three things Tretiak can do in the current social/political situation. He must either *a*, take over the country, *b*, go out and get hit by a bus, or *c,* be put out of business by the two of us. If he does *a,* everyone except him will be miserable. If he does *b,* we'll be saved a great deal of trouble and hard work."

"I vote for *b,*" she interjected, "and the sooner the better."

"I don't believe we can count on *b* as a realistic expectation," commented Templar politely.

She drained the dark bottom of her plastic coffee cup and eyed her visitor.

"What makes you think *c* is more realistic? Toli said one word and—" Her voice caught in her throat and she clenched her jaw.

Simon came around the counter and put a warm and welcome hand on her shoulder.

"Put your faith in me, Frankie. We can do it."

She wanted to believe him, wanted to pin her hopes and dreams on this charismatic buccaneer who offered no assurances beyond his own dynamic personality.

"Other men have tried," commented Frankie as if she were attempting to tease, "stronger men, braver men . . ."

"Assuming for the moment that such men ever existed," interrupted Templar with slightly forced joviality, "you've never met anyone luckier or more daring than I. With your help, we can melt Tretiak's plot like last year's snow."

She ordered her lips to smile while her eyes glistened. "We make it hot for that rat, Tretiak?"

Absolutely," confirmed Simon.

"You got some secret rat remover formula or something?"

Templar smiled and patted his coat pocket. "As a matter of fact, Frankie, my secret formula arrived a half-hour ago by fax. I'm being straight with you. This is a country under reconstruction. Together we'll make a positive contribution to the collective effort of re-modeling and beautification."

The mansion of Ivan Tretiak was the only comfort-ably heated home in Moscow, and it, too, was under construction. A daily army of workers, staff, and clean-ing women swarmed over the estate while Tretiak, Ilya, and their crooked compatriots plotted the over-throw of the government.

Despite the depleted coal supplies, the tragic and supposedly inexplicable demise of Russia's hydroelec-tric plants, the lack of natural gas lines except in the most prestigious diplomatic neighborhoods, and the much touted oil shortage, Tretiak enjoyed all the com-forts of a well-heated domicile.

He also enjoyed the taste of black caviar and the aroma of impending victory while discussing strategies with the edgy General Sklarov. Ilya attempted ap-pearing important, mostly by barking orders at the cleaning crew.

"I can count on my troops," asserted the general, "but I was led to believe you'd soon unveil a great miracle to galvanize the mob."

Tretiak waved his hand as if all of this were of no concern. He crunched a cracker smeared with dark fish roe and spoke with his mouth full.

"Like the Miracle of Communism, the Miracle of Cold Fusion failed." He moistened his mouth with a gulp of vodka. "But it doesn't matter. We have duped Karpov one way or another. If our recent ruse worked, we will get billions out of him before we strike. The stink of failure will be all over him, not me. Before he can scrub it off, you mobilize the army and together we take over."

Tretiak brushed crumbs from his shirt as the general helped himself to more caviar.

Sklarov's many years in Russia's military had taught him all manner of duplicity and corruption. His clandestine support of Tretiak, coupled with a dedicated legion of Special Forces within the military itself, placed him in a delicate yet powerful position.

"You realize that once the coup is attempted, it must be swift and victorious, not like that botched attempt a few years back," insisted Sklarov.

Tretiak chewed and gloated. He had it all figured out.

"I promised Karpov that the opposition would cease if he funded cold fusion." Tretiak laughed. "But once the billions are in my pocket, what can he do? Every night the demonstrations become bigger, more violent, and the citizens are too cold to think clearly. When the time is right, we will synchronize a massive rally and media event with the sudden strike of your Special Forces." Tretiak's voice boomed with confidence and megalomania. "Within an hour or less, all of Russia and its vast resources and power will be ours!"

Tretiak halted his diatribe when a stooped old babushka from the cleaning crew shuffled in and waved a feather duster over an antique loveseat.

Ilya immediately asserted his illusory authority.

"Not now, old witch! We're working! Git before I boot your ancient ass outa here!"

She turned and humbly scooted out, but not before dropping a subminiature microphone-transmitter not much bigger than a dust mote onto the bookshelf behind the conspirators.

With the mission accomplished, the stooped and disguised Simon Templar hurried down the hall, ducked into a doorway, and concealed himself in what was obviously Ilya's room.

Hip-Hop CDs, porno magazines, and "white power" propaganda were scattered across the floor. In the corner, leaning against the wall, was Ilya's walking stick.

Templar stared at it, remembering Tretiak's pompous warning:

"We could kill you and stroll away, even here in this transit lounge. . . ."

A quick, careful examination of the tapered tip revealed a retractable needle which, if augmented with poison, would be discreetly lethal.

"Walking death," murmured the Saint.

Returning his concentration to the tasks at hand, Templar stole a peek out the doorway. He saw a newly delivered shipment of chemicals being carried upstairs by a liveried servant.

As for Ilya, he stood in the foyer sniffing the air like a dog. There was something about the old woman that unnerved him, something naggingly familiar.

Templar striped off his rags. Beneath them he wore a painter's outfit. He stuffed the babushka disguise in a formerly concealed gallon paint can and reemerged into the main area of the mansion. When the servant descended the stairs and Ilya had moved on, Templar went up to Botvin's lab.

The little scientist was dispiritedly hooking a length of palladium wire to a electrolyte cell when he heard the creak of the opening door.

"You're not allowed in here," Botvin told the painter in Russian. "All the work is out there."

"The work could be in here, you know," said Templar in English as he maneuvered to get a better look at Botvin's setup.

"You better go quick, whoever you are," advised the nervous physicist, attempting to block Templar's view.

"You're not really doing anything up here except playing with lightbulbs. This is a sham—a bad Tretiak joke on the same folks who've pinned their hopes on him. You know it and I know it."

Botvin was close to tears. He didn't know what to say, or to whom he would be saying it.

"Nothing but props," continued Templar evenly. "But you wish they worked with all your heart, don't you? Isn't that what you *really* want?"

"My heart? No . . . with all my *dusha*, my soul . . . people are freezing to death, you know."

"Not in this house, I notice," remarked Templar. He held up the faxed printout of Emma's cold fusion formula.

"Look at this and tell me if it means anything to you."

Botvin squinted at the paper. His glasses began to fog.

He answered, and his voice was a constricted whisper.

"It clarifies Dr. Russell's seven cards . . . How did you get this? Who are you?"

Templar's eyes seemed to pierce Botvin's lenses.

"A friend of Dr. Russell's, which also means I'm no friend of your boss—and neither are you. In truth, you're a man of science, not brute force."

Botvin gingerly took the printout and began reading it carefully. When he spoke, it was in subdued, awed tones.

"For the first time, I think I understand what she was getting at. . . ."

Botvin's pure heart pounded in his chest. He thought not of fame or glory, but only of his freezing countrymen.

"Will you try to make it work?"

"Every hour of every day!" insisted the scientist. "To think, a future free from the tyranny of winter!" He quickly turned to his computer, his mind racing. "I'll need some time alone. . . ."

"Work well and work fast," advised the Saint. "Your boss plans to discredit Karpov with cold fusion's failure at a Red Square rally."

Both men heard the noise of someone ascending the staircase.

Templar quickly handed Botvin a two-way transmitter-receiver not much larger than the bug he left on Tretiak's bookshelf.

"Now that we're friends," asserted Templar, "let's stay in touch."

Botvin nodded and placed it in his pocket just as the door opened and Ilya entered. He barely noticed the busy painter slipping past, calling out details of paint requirements in a deep Russian baritone.

"Botvin, you useless intellectual," snapped Ilya, "have you seen a filthy old babushka?"

"It is not my job to keep track of your women, Little Ilya," remarked Botvin coldly. "Now, please, I have had enough interruptions for one day. I am doing important work for your father, for Russia."

Ilya's Doc Martens stomped out of the room and back down the stairs.

Tretiak continued his conspiratorial conversation in the library, unaware that every incriminating morsel of conversation was being clearly transmitted and recorded, including an unexpected telephone call from President Karpov.

Informed by Vereshagin that Karpov was on the line, Tretiak began to gloat.

"I can almost feel my bank account straining under the weight of all those billions," he joked before picking up the receiver.

"Because you came to me with these cold fusion plans as a patriot," began Karpov warmly, "and because you have the best interests of Russia at heart . . ."

Tretiak smiled broadly, cradled the phone against his shoulder, and spread himself a caviar-covered celebratory cracker.

"Yes, true, true," agreed Tretiak before taking a bite.

"I propose, as a patriot, also," continued the president, "that you sell your cold fusion to the Chinese—it would be good fun to watch those old farts lose eighty-two billion yen!"

Tretiak stopped chewing mid-bite.

"According to my experts who've reviewed your data," continued Karpov in the same tone, "I'd do as well to buy blueprints for a perpetual-motion machine. Or better yet, a skyhook!"

Tretiak spit his mouthfull of cracker and caviar into a napkin.

"Your experts lead you down a path of weakness, of feminine submission," countered Tretiak angrily. "Soon Mother Russia will be gang-raped by Western Europe while America looks on, giggling . . . her corpse picked cleaner than by Napoleon and Hitler combined!"

Karpov, unruffled, replied.

"You have a gift for the mixed malign metaphor, but as a salesman, you're a failure."

"History is littered with would-be leaders who failed to act at the decisive moment. . . ." Tretiak ranted.

"Oh, I'm decisive," interrupted President Karpov. "I've decided to terminate this conversation."

Tretiak was left holding a silent telephone.

He hung up, shrugged, and poured himself a fresh drink.

"No matter," he said with a smile. "After the coup, the billions will be ours anyway."

Vereshagin, Sklarov, and Tretiak raised their glasses in a toast to their glorious, victorious future.

Simultaneously Templar, appearing no different than any number of painters and workmen swarming over the mansion, took the liberty of exploration. He cheerfully let himself into every room of Tretiak's domicile, and contented himself that he had cased the joint with thoroughness and professionalism.

Then, in Tretiak's private master suite, he was struck by inspiration. Unlike other Russians, Tretiak had heat. He also had hot water.

He actually did it—he walked casually into the master bath and turned on the tap. Ten minutes later, while Tretiak and his co-conspirators were revealing all to a hidden microphone, Simon Templar was stretched full length in a steaming bathtub, innocently playing submarine with the sponge and a bar of soap.

Later, towel dried and freshly scrubbed, the paint crew's extra man simply exited the mansion and rendezvoused with Frankie. Together, they listened to the recorded conversation crackling over a cheap tape recorder speaker in her sparse, barracks-like apartment, to Tretiak's voice:

"Karpov is such a fool. No one's guessed the simple truth of where the heating oil went." Tretiak laughed as he clinked fresh ice into his drink. "Those 'in the know' think I sold it abroad. The liberal press has been hunting for a paper trail that doesn't exist."

The gloating distorted laughter was too much for even the Templar to stomach. He reached past Frankie and flicked off the machine.

"Tretiak's morals are lamentably defective from whatever angle they're viewed," muttered Templar. "I need a moment with President Karpov. The old KGB must've built tunnels under the president's home, and I bet someone as clever as you would have the map."

Frankie emitted a harsh laugh, then crossed to the window where she's stuffed fresh, dry newspaper into the cracks to keep out the bitter Russian wind. She uncrumpled page one of *Ekho Moskvv* and translated the headline. " 'Embattled President Retreats Behind Kremlin Walls. Under siege from critics and freezing populace, Karpov has moved today from his home to a sanctuary behind barricades.' "

Templar seemed unconcerned.

"Then I'll break into the Kremlin."

Frankie's jaw dropped in stunned incredulity.

"That's crazy! You kid, yes?"

"I have a highly refined sense of humor," he acknowledged, "but I kid you not."

Frankie gulped and shook her head.

"You amaze me. I don't know if you brave or crazy or both."

"Probably both," said Templar pleasantly. "You drive, yes?"

"Better than any cabbie," she bragged. "I even have a classic Zhiguli motorcycle complete with sidecar."

"Sounds a bit chilly for this weather."

"So, you got a car?"

"Frankie, my dear," said Templar as he placed a warm hand on her shoulder, "I'm the man who has everything."

"You rich or something?"

Simon sat down at her worn table. They could see their breath in the air.

"Sit down, Frankie. I have something to tell you."

She regarded him warily.

"No, really it's fine, sit down."

She sat.

"I'm rich. Very rich. Ridiculously rich."

Frankie's smile increased in expansion with each repetition of the word *rich*.

"How very very ridiculous rich?"

"How rich is rich to you, Frankie?"

She looked around the simple and frigid apartment.

"With all my hustle, all my icons and replicas and tourists, this is the best I can do. And I don't do it all for me, you know. And not just Toli, may God rest his soul, but . . ."

The smile in her eyes was betrayed by the tear in her voice.

"There are others in this building we care, I mean . . . without Toli . . . I care for . . ."

She became shy at the topic of her own generosity.

"I'm not such a big tough cookie as I pretend sometimes, yes?"

Templar recalled her returning the Bulgari Chronograph.

"So, you ask me how rich is rich to me," she said

thoughtfully. Frankie stroked her chin as if she had a beard, which she certainly did not.

"A million dollars American money would be more than anyone I know could imagine. You have that much?" The lilt in her voice was admittedly hopeful.

Templar smiled, for Frankie had only a veneer of guile, a slick outer coating of opportunism. She was, by her own reluctant admission, selfless.

"Let me take you to dinner, Frankie. And I mean the fanciest restaurant in all of Moscow."

"Oh, I am so sure of that! I could not. Not me."

Templar laughed and his breath made warm clouds in the air. "Why not?"

"I might like it or think I deserved it, for one thing," she explained. "Or you may think you get more than friendship and justice, no?"

"No," clarified Templar, "my motives are pure, really. Besides, my appetite is coming back."

She looked at him in a way that caught him off guard, for her eyes seemed to read his very soul.

She took his hand. "I think you are a very rich man, like you say. And maybe that's more than a million American dollars, or two million—"

"Or fifty million plus mounting compound interest."

"Wow! Fifty million. Plus interest mounting. Well, no matter," continued Frankie. "I believe you because you don't know, or maybe forgot, about being poor."

"I've been poor, Frankie. I was raised in a Hong Kong orphanage until I was thirteen."

"You Chinese? Part, at least I think, yes?"

"I think, yes. Some. I don't look very Chinese, but you've heard of Mendel's Law?"

"I probably broke that one, too," said Frankie, and Templar suppressed a smile. "But the point, Mr.

Templar Rich Man is this: For what you spend on two meals at fancy place in Moscow, I could feed the families in this building. You buy me big meal, I would choke on it thinking of the people here. You understand?"

"Let's order out," chirped Templar.

"Order what?"

Templar stood with an expansive gesture. "I hear that in Russia, everything is unavailable. Unless you have money. Then, everything is very available. True?"

Frankie rolled her eyes. It was too true.

"I provide the money, you go shopping. We'll have a big meal and invite the neighbors—we feed them all. If you can find an electric space heater, buy a few of those, too."

Frankie's eyes grew larger and larger. "You're not kidding?"

Templar tossed an absurd amount of cash in her lap. "I trust you, Frankie. Let's eat."

Simon Templar knew he was fumbling at friendship. At worst, he was buying it. At best, he was practicing it.

The thick flakes fell in hefty blankets over the city of Moscow, and it was not long after Templar extended his offer that they returned to her apartment building from a thrill-packed visit to a decidedly clandestine supermarket.

Bag after bag of groceries and goodies were hauled in, much to the delight of the many invited guests.

Doors between apartments were propped ajar, and soon the heady aroma of sizzling meat, cooking cabbage, and sautéed onions blended with the laughter and camaraderie of the about-to-be well fed.

Samovars were heated, tea was brewed, and Templar basked in a warmth beyond coal or oil. He had not allowed himself the luxury of honest companionship in decades, and the pleasure of its simplicity ignited a spark within him.

Frankie resisted showing off her rich friend as one would a carnival prize, and instead introduced him as a long-time acquaintance and occasional business partner. She said that they made a lucrative sale to a busload of wealthy tourists.

The resultant feast was, according to Frankie, a celebration of capitalistic family values.

"I hear that phrase from jerk Tretiak when he gave big speech in Red Square," she said with a wink.

Templar was joyously introduced to a wide array of lower-middle-class apartment dwellers, most of them exceptionally pleasant and delightfully hospitable.

He played a few hands of gin rummy with the enchanting Olya from Chelyabinsk, a natural beauty who was on her way to becoming a consummate cardsharp.

"Watch out for that one," warned Frankie with a giddy laugh. "She graduated with honors from Language Lycee ninety-three, and someday she will marry my cousin!"

"Gin!" exclaimed Olya.

"Warn your cousin," advised Templar.

They ate, they laughed, they sipped tea and enjoyed each other's company. For those few brief hours Simon Templar allowed himself to escape into a world he had only seen from the outside—a world of honest friends and unselfish sharing.

When the last members of the impromptu dinner

party had eaten their fill and returned to their own subdivided cubicles, Frankie finished her tea and eyed Templar quizzically.

"Okay, we all ate. Now what?"

Templar chuckled and sat down opposite her. "I had a marvelous time."

"Yeah. Me, too. When do you see the president?" Back to business.

"Oh, that's easy," replied Templar. "When I break into the Kremlin."

"You'd have to be world's best burglar to do that. . . ."

"True," agreed Templar.

Frankie narrowed her eyes and stared at him.

"What exactly do you do?"

"Let me put it this way, Frankie: Scotland Yard says I can break into anywhere. They don't like me much. They don't know my name, but they call me the Saint."

Frankie smirked. "I don't see halo over your head," she said. "The police are looking for you everywhere, this is true?"

"They won't find me here, now, will they?"

"Scotland Yard doesn't come here very often," she said with a nonchalant shrug. "Besides, you don't seem like criminal to me. Tretiak is criminal."

"Well, Frankie, I guess I was a criminal. I've had somewhat of a change of heart, or modification of career, or reorientation of identity." He laughed aloud as if he was enjoying a marvelous joke.

She looked at him curiously.

"Someone tell a funny story and I missed it?"

"Yes," continued Templar enthusiastically, "it's the funniest story of my life, a grand and glorious adventure. Consider me a finely tempered sword slowly becoming unsheathed."

"No unsheathing around me, please," admonished Frankie with a wag of her finger. "We just friends. Now, you plan to stop Tretiak's takeover or you going to have more dessert?"

The Saint had more dessert. Frankie stared at him.

"I don't rush into things, Frankie. I plan, and I plan well. And you are a very lucky woman."

"I am?"

"Indeed," replied Templar happily. "You are about to see a world-class expert at the top of his form."

"Hoo-boychic," she said wearily. "I hope you as wonderful as you think."

2

ANY DOUBTS LINGERING IN FRANKIE'S MIND CONCERN-
ing Simon Templar's abilities evaporated in the heat
of first-hand experience. The next several hours were
the busiest and most memorable of her life.

It was Frankie who emptied Templar's locker at the
train station, and she managed to suppress an audible
gasp when she saw the quantity of cash, diversity of
passports, and high-tech toys stashed therein.

It was Frankie who then sought out the self-sacrificing
Sofiya. Perched on her high-heels and eyeing the street
for her next cash customer, the plucky teenager's first
response to Frankie's approach was polite but firm.

"No ladies," she said with a shake of her head.

"That's not what this is about," Frankie assured her
and handed over an envelope.

"Take this upstairs before you open it, and don't
tell anyone how you got it."

Sofiya accepted it with curiosity, took it to her apartment, and tore open the clasp.

Inside was more money than she had ever seen in her life and a small scrap of paper containing two words: THANK YOU.

"Mama," called out Sofiya, "I just retired!"

It was Frankie who nervously drove the mirror-windowed minivan—she didn't have the nerve to ask Templar where it came from—while the Saint snapped photos of the Kremlin through the silvered panes.

"Kremlin no savings bank or museum like you usually rob, Famous Templar," advised Frankie. "The word *Kremlin* means 'fortified stronghold.'"

"I've done my homework," murmured Templar as he snapped more photos. "Karpov's Kremlin is ninety acres enclosed by a 1.4-mile brick wall built during the reign of Grand Duke Ivan the Third back in the mid 1400s. The Kremlin stopped being a fortress in the seventeenth century."

"Tell that to the guards, motion sensors, and surveillance cameras," suggested Frankie. "I like that Karpov," she added seriously. "He tried to do good things. Too bad politics such dirty business."

"A universal problem. Partisan politics is, by its very nature, divisive. Tretiak wants to divide it all into his pocket, his power, and he doesn't care who freezes in the process."

The van's windshield wipers sloshed aside a fresh layer of icy snow.

"Why you taking all these pictures when you can buy postcards like any other tourist?"

"A mental exercise," explained Templar. "I always take pictures of the target."

"Wouldn't you rather have a map of Stalin's bunker?"

Simon stopped his index finger in mid-snap.

"Did you say . . . ?"

Frankie smiled.

"I told you before, I *am* the Russian underground."

Within the Kremlin walls, the oldest ensemble was centered around the Cathedral Square. It consisted of the Assumption Cathedral, where rulers were crowned, the Annunciation Cathedral, private church of the tzars, the Archangel Cathedral, burial place of the royal family until Tsar Peter I, the Hall of the Facets with a magnificent vaulted throne room, and the 266-foot Bell Tower of Ivan III.

None of these astonishing structures, rich in history and packed with priceless artifacts, were of significant interest to Simon Templar. He was far more concerned with the labyrinth of tunnels below ground— tunnels detailed in the dozens of maps spread out in Frankie's underground art lair.

The authentic replicas, fabricated artifacts, and other bits of fakery were shoved out of the way. One hundred percent of their concentration was focused on finding a way into Stalin's bunker.

"Look. Lead-lined door reinforced with eight feet of concrete," explained Frankie, poking her finger at a particular illustration. "Maybe you take nuclear weapon with you in tunnel and blow yourself up inside?"

"Not a practical solution." Simon Templar sighed. "But if there is a door, that means there is a way for the door to open."

"Sure. See that sensor on the entrance hatch?"

Templar squinted in the yellow light from the lair's oil lamps. "More or less."

"It's a radiation detector. It will only open the door after dissipation of nuclear fallout," she explained, as if such details were common knowledge. "It's very sophisticated, very intelligent. It was updated during Gorbachev's time. The idea is that if you hide in there during nuclear war, when fallout goes away, the door opens."

Templar marveled at the concept.

"Put this in a penny-dreadful pot-boiler and no one would swallow it for a second."

Frankie had no idea what Templar was talking about.

"That means you're cooked? You giving up this crazy idea?"

He smiled his most seraphic and illuminating smile. "Of course not. If this system is intelligent, that means it can think. If it can think, it can be fooled."

"Well, you have me fooled," agreed Frankie, and took a peek at Simon's Bulgari Chronograph. "Can you trick the door of Stalin's bunker, get into the Kremlin, and warn Karpov before General Sklarov's Special Forces help Tretiak take over?"

A serious question.

"That has been a primary concern," acknowledged the Saint.

"Maybe you should just call Karpov on the telephone. That be easier."

Templar laughed and ran his hands through his hair. "Why Frankie, what adventure is there in that? Besides, President Karpov has an unlisted number. Crawling around under the Kremlin will be good exercise for both of us."

Frankie gulped.

"Both . . . ?"

"Of course, I treasure your companionship."

"Am I supposed to say thank you?"

"You're supposed to brew some warm tea while I perform high-tech miracles and assemble my wardrobe."

"Wardrobe?"

"The play's the thing, Frankie," said Templar happily, pulling digital toys out of a knapsack, "and I have a costume for every occasion."

She put a kettle on the small propane stove and shook her head in amazement. She had already seen the rather astonishing contents of his garment bag.

"You're a different kind of man, all right. Maybe you should go into politics."

"Heaven forbid," admonished Templar playfully as he scanned portions of the Kremlin ground-plan onto a three-inch square card. "Besides, Tretiak might hear you, and you know what he thinks of competition."

She shrugged and poured the hot water. "Tretiak big rat. Sklarov big rat. Karpov . . . I don't know . . . maybe a mouse—a democratic mouse. But up there, outside, the people getting more mad; army getting more scary."

She paused as if remembering something, then reached under the counter and lifted up a tiny black-and-white portable television.

"Runs on handful of D batteries," Frankie explained, switching it on. "Reception not great, but . . ."

She stood in the lamplight, shadows of concern casting lines across her face, listening to the news report of another of Tretiak's Oktober Party rallies.

General Sklarov's voice crackled over the small speaker while the on-screen image wavered back and forth.

". . . three great empires have dominated the world: Rome, Constantinople, and Russia. All three have fallen. Only one can be restored, and only one man can restore it—Ivan Tretiak!"

A thunderous response of stamping feet drowned out Sklarov's shouted repetition of Tretiak's name.

"When the world going to learn?" asked Frankie. "One more crook. One more dictator. One more liar. How many people die to make one more rich man even more rich?"

The crowd cheered as Tretiak himself took the microphone.

"You know me, I am Ivan Tretiak—a lunatic, a dreamer, a poet—a lunatic because I'm haunted by the fantasy of an empire that reclaims her former might, a dreamer beset by nightmares of the West cackling as it castrates us in the name of democracy, a poet spinning rhymes of Russia not cut off at the knees, but armed to the teeth! Not ridiculed, but revered!"

The crowd erupted in abject cacophonia.

"No, more than revered," shouted Tretiak, *"feared!"*

Pandemonium. Tretiak continued, speaking over the clamor, his voice rising steadily.

"President Karpov will hand you over, weak and frozen, to the Western liberals, foreigners, and one-worlders, but it is not too late. We do not need to re-create Russia, we need to re-arm Russia! Russia is not a sweet old babushka who's seen better days. No! Soon the babushka will rip off her rags, rear up, and reveal that she is Mother Russia, roaring bear!"

The crowd was in a frenzy.

"The world had better cringe from her claws!"

The hoarse, frenzied howl rising from the maddened crowd seemed to throb with a horrible blood lust.

Then came the music, the rhythm, and the synchronized juggernaut tramp of marching men.

Frankie shuddered and turned down the volume.

"It's horrible," she said sadly, "horrible."

Templar set his jaw for a moment, and when he spoke his voice was curiously low. Frankie could almost hear the rumble of iron on the streets above.

"You understand, Frankie, but millions don't. Whole nations that call themselves intelligent human beings are perfectly willing to exchange their brains for a brass band and tax themselves to starvation to buy bigger and better bombs. Were that not the case, criminals like Tretiak would never get anywhere. Brass and drums, Frankie, brass and drums and the thunder of marching feet—that's what this country is about to succumb to, and that's a fate colder and more deadly than any oil shortage."

"Where does this all lead, Simon. What if we can't stop it?"

"I'll tell you exactly where it leads—streets swarming with uniformed militia, neighbors betraying neighbors, midnight arrests, the third degree, secret tribunals, forced confessions, kangaroo courts, concentration camps, firing squads."

Frankie sat down wearily. "Sounds familiar."

"Too familiar," agreed Templar. "It's the description of a world gone mad—a world divided against itself."

Frankie managed something resembling a hopeful smile.

"Hey, you sound like one of those one-world people Tretiak doesn't like, either."

Templar smiled back. "Well, if you don't like the idea of one world, how many worlds do you want, and how would you like them divided? By race? By religion? By income? Unless you have a spare planet in your pocket, one world is all we have."

"And you think you can save the world, Simon Templar?"

At that moment, had he answered in the affirmative, she would have believed him without question. There was a strange fire in his ice-blue eyes, and a rakish line to his features that bespoke confidence and victory.

"No. Not the world. Not today, Frankie," said Templar, "but you and I together are going to do our best to save this one little part of it."

"One frozen part of it," added Frankie, pulling her collar up around her chin. She pointed up toward the ceiling. "Going to be pretty hot in Red Square tomorrow."

Frankie's prophetic utterance was based on simple logical deduction of available facts—the same facts reiterated less than twenty-four hours later to their respective audiences by CNN's Jan Sharp and UPN's Chet Rogers, both broadcasting from Red Square.

"As freezing temperatures and fuel shortages continue to take their lethal toll," reported Sharp, "and rumors sweep Moscow that many more deaths are unreported—troops under the command of right-wing General Leo Sklarov have begun to ring the Russian capital."

Rogers, situated more precariously amidst the throng than Sharp, spoke with an edge of self-concern in his manly baritone. "Angry, frightened citizens are flocking to Red Square at this hour, but this time they are not braving the bitter cold for another political rally turned riot—they've been drawn here by the promise of a 'revelation' to be displayed on these colossal video screens. . . ."

The video screens to which the reporter referred were the same shimmering technological marvels utilized by Tretiak in all his previous rallies—screens that made him seem larger than life and transformed him into an enormous, electronically enhanced champion of the people.

"This has become a life-and-death struggle," exclaimed the hyperbole-laced reporter, "an intense drama played out on a very large stage whose final curtain is yet to come!"

Accompanying the intense drama were equally intense sound effects. The thunderous roar of stomping feet on concrete rumbled through the ground and vibrated the earth above Templar and Frankie, who were making their way through the dark and dismal tunnels beneath Red Square.

"Eek," squeaked Frankie, and she waved her flashlight wildly.

"Eek? I can't believe you actually said 'Eek.'"

Frankie sidestepped another enormous rodent.

"How these rats get so big! There's nothing down here but dirt, rats, and bigger rats—well, and you and me."

Simon smiled in the darkness, his steady flashlight beam shining on the three-inch square card onto which he had scanned a detailed multilevel Kremlin ground-plan.

"That gizmo should be right around here somewhere," he remarked as he tucked the card into his breast pocket, "and it should be pretty obvious."

"As obvious as *that?*" Frankie's beam found a massive set of concrete slabs.

Templar examined the detection unit. It was encased in steel mesh and recessed in the concrete. He knelt down, unshouldered his backpack, and removed a Plexiglas box and cordless bolt-driver.

"Here's where we play 'fool the gizmo,' Frankie. This box has two compartments—one empty and one with radon gas. . . ."

He began bolting it over the radiation detector. With the box snugly in place, he turned a little knob, which opened the divider between the compartments.

Frankie strained to see every detail.

"The gas is released, the sensor will sense it, and you and I will pray that it can't tell the difference between radon and plutonium," said Templar.

"Oh." Frankie was not sure she understood. "Well, I don't know the difference, if that helps."

The detector's emergency light began blinking.

"The gizmo thinks it just survived a nuclear attack," explained Templar happily as he used the bolt driver to loosen the box. "Now it thinks it's several months later . . . Moscow is rebuilding from the rubble . . ." He pulled the box away, dissipating the gas. ". . . and the radiation is gone."

The emergency light stopped blinking, there was a low rumble, and the concrete slab slid open. Behind it was a simple, old-fashioned padlocked door.

The Saint chuckled. "I could open this thing with a stickpin."

He didn't have a stickpin, but he did have his multi-purpose penknife.

Templar and Frankie eased themselves into the dank, dusty compartment, unchanged since World War II. There was even an old strategic map tacked to the wall.

"Stalin's bunker," whispered Frankie in awe. "It sure is dirty."

"Well, places like this are hard to keep up," offered Templar. He squinted at his square card. "The stairs should be . . ."

"There," said Frankie with finality. "The stairs leading to the artesian well are right there."

A moment of uncomfortable silence passed between them.

"Thank you, Frankie. Honestly, I couldn't have made it this far without you."

"Don't get killed, Mr. Famous Templar."

He gave her a hug and it was awkward for both of them.

"With any luck," joked the Saint, "I'll never see you again. And if my luck is bad . . ."

Frankie laughed and touched his shoulder before she turned back toward the tunnel.

"I'll be waiting on the edge of Red Square with a souped-up motorcycle—vintage 1953," said Frankie with a laugh. "And you know what, Mr. Templar? You're a sentimental fool after all."

Her light disappeared.

Templar turned his attention to the stairs. He took a deep breath and steeled himself. He was in his element—the odds were against him, the stakes were high, and he was all confidence.

3

THE KREMLIN'S SOOTY BASEMENT CONTAINED A MULTI-
tude of machines dating from the Industrial Revolution slaving away with more noise than efficiency,
humming and throbbing like the bowels of some me-
chanical behemoth.

It was from between these gear-grinding, steam-
emitting relics that Simon Templar emerged. He had
scaled the stairs, pulled himself up through the well
opening, and became fairly sooty himself in the
process.

He stripped off his darkly stained overcoat, revealing a perfectly starched and gleaming Kremlin guard
uniform.

"Just like in the movies," said Templar to himself
as he tossed the overcoat down the well. "Now it's
time to meet and mingle."

If Templar was on schedule, so was the attempted

coup. From a hastily acquired vantage point in an above-ground corridor, he saw Sklarov's Special Forces penetrating the grounds without opposition—proof that Sklarov had allies within the Kremlin guard itself. Soon General Sklarov would enter the Presidential Residence unhindered.

Templar quickly oriented himself on his ground-plan card, and began marching toward Karpov's apartments as if he were following orders. There would be authentic Kremlin guards to deal with, but he had come well prepared.

Approaching the apartments, Templar slid behind a baroque pillar and waited—he didn't wait long.

A genuine Kremlin guard rounded the corner. As he passed the pillar, Templar quickly seized him from behind and pressed an ether-soaked rag over the man's face. He collapsed, unconscious, as a second guard came into view.

Templar called out in Russian as he hurried farther down the hall. "He's had a seizure! I'll get help!"

It took the second guard a moment to realize that he had never seen Templar before. Once the realization hit, his sidearm was aimed at the Saint.

"Sdavaites!"

Templar paid no heed to the guard's call for surrender, but whirled around brandishing a pistol of his own. He shot one perfectly aimed round at the chandelier above the guard's head. It shattered in a barrage of falling crystal, and the guard ducked for cover.

Alerted by the shot, a squadron of guards ran toward the sound. By the time they arrived, Simon Templar had daringly thrown himself into President Karpov's private bedroom.

Startled awake, Karpov shielded his terrified wife

with his own body. His eyes strained to focus on the man barricading the door.

Simon switched on the lights and held up his open palms toward the shocked and agitated president.

"I'm here to warn you, Mr. President, not harm you. You're in danger, but not from me."

"Get out!" yelled Karpov. "I could have you killed!"

"Sklarov's Special Forces have mounted a coup," explained Templar. "He's on his way here right now."

The president sat bolt upright while his wife pulled the sheets back up under her chin.

"Why wasn't I—"

"Warned? Because many of your own Kremlin guards take orders from Sklarov," declared Templar.

Muffled orders could be heard from the hall outside.

"I'm unhurt," shouted Karpov, fearing his intruder was telling the truth. "Back off and leave us alone. If I need you, I'll call you. Go away."

His guards, reluctantly obedient, complied.

The Saint moved closer. His voice was even and nonthreatening.

"It's all Tretiak's work, Mr. President. How do you think this heating crisis came to exist?"

Karpov hid his head in his hands; his wife hid under the covers.

"It's a nightmare, a dreadful combination of natural disasters, worker rebellion, and treachery by Tretiak!"

Templar sat down pleasantly on the edge of the bed.

"Natural disasters? Worker rebellion? President Karpov, you and I both know that Russia is richer in natural resources than any other country on earth— the world's largest coal fields are here, as are vast deposits of petroleum . . ."

"Our coal processing abilities were crippled by the severe damage of earthquakes, and that damn Tretiak sold off our oil reserves to the West! If I could only find proof . . ."

Templar shook his head in negative sympathy.

"The coal crisis happened, conveniently enough, when Tretiak was minister of energy. He's been planning this ruse for a long time, and I'm positive that he hasn't sold a drop of oil to anyone. He's been hoarding it himself."

Karpov looked intently at the Saint, studying his face.

"Mr. President, the time is short," insisted the Saint. "The coup is on, and Tretiak intends to humiliate you."

Karpov's face blanched; his wife trembled so hard it shook the bed.

"You didn't force your way in here to tell me something I can do nothing about," said Karpov, his plaintive expression far from presidential. "Do you have a brilliant suggestion?"

Templar smiled his most luminous smile, and his bright blue eyes gleamed with almost childlike mischief.

"Now that you mention it, a good-hearted scientist named Lev Botvin and I were discussing your dilemma only recently. You're going to stand trial before the world in Red Square tonight. Whatever Tretiak accuses you of, admit to it."

The president of Russia and the man at the top of Inspector Teal's "Most Wanted" list had an intense and productive meeting of the minds. It would have gone on longer, but the bedroom door being suddenly blown off its hinges was a loud and effective interruption.

It was Sklarov. His Special Forces had overwhelmed the Kremlin guards by force of numbers and significant internal collusion. Not a shot was fired.

The gloating renegade general, his chest puffed out and his head held high, walked triumphantly into the president's bedroom accompanied by two of his larger and more ominous men.

"My, my, my," declared Sklarov, "what an interesting sight—the president, his wife, and a Kremlin guard. Too bad I forgot my camera."

Karpov attempted sounding authoritative, but his reclining position and bedtime attire undermined his effort.

"What you're attempting is illegal! The people won't stand for it!"

Sklarov hacked out a rude laugh. "The people are too cold to stop it." He snapped instructions. "Leave Mrs. Karpov here under guard, detain the former president downstairs, but let him get dressed first. He'd look too sympathetic and pathetic standing outside in his pajamas."

Sklarov turned to appraise Simon Templar. "Who are you?"

"I'm Edmund Campion," he replied, "named for the saint tried on false charges of treason."

Sklarov ripped the epaulets from Templar's uniform. "Isn't a saint someone who dies horribly?"

"That's a martyr," said Templar helpfully. "A saint is someone who can be linked to three miracles."

Mrs. Karpov peeked out over the bedspread.

Sklarov snorted and gave orders to his Special Forces. "He wants a miracle. Make him disappear!"

Not content to simply drag Templar from the room, the two Special Forces thugs gave him several body blows from their rifle butts before hauling him out the door.

"Your boss didn't say anything about hitting me," insisted Templar. "Who gave you guys the latitude to improvise?"

They ignored him.

As they roughly escorted Templar down the corridor, they came face-to-face with Ilya.

Templar was as surprised to see him as he was to see the Saint.

"What are *you* doing here?" Ilya was incredulous. "Why are you meddling in our politics when you could be out stealing something?"

"It's not politics," stated Templar flatly, "it's personal."

Sklarov was approaching, and Ilya wanted to appear powerful. After all, he had outfitted himself in full blackshirt regalia in honor of the triumphant coup.

"Let's drag him out with the former president," ordered Ilya. He escorted the heavily guarded captive down the hall, gloating with every step. "In a few minutes, the mob will tear you and the president limb from limb. And then, with busybodies and do-gooders done away with, Russia belongs to us."

Templar begged to differ.

"No, Russia belongs to Daddy."

If the Saint was baiting, Ilya wasn't biting.

"True, Ivan Tretiak will rule with a mightier hand than any Russian tzar since Ivan the Terrible."

"Interesting analogy," said the Saint. "You know Ivan the Terrible killed his own son."

Ilya, proudly striding, missed a step.

"Yes, by his own hand," Templar continued conversationally. "The boy was just about your age, I believe. . . ."

"Shut up!"

Simon smiled, Ilya scowled, and the soldiers led Templar out toward Red Square.

"Get ready for your final minutes of fame, Templar," spat Ilya. "You're going to be a featured player in our final big show."

The "big show" to which Ilya referred was another one of Tretiak's choreographed media events. Only the addition of a juggler spinning plates, trained seals tooting horns, or dancing bears doing the Lambada could have made it more viewer-friendly.

The two giant video screens were filled with inflammatory Oktober Party propaganda, and Red Square itself was crowded with the irate, the curious, and the soon-to-be condemned.

International news correspondents from the major networks cupped their ears and rattled details into their open microphones, bringing every rumor and unconfirmed charge to their world-wide audiences.

"In an emergency measure approved by the Russian Senate, all documents in President Karpov's Kremlin office have been seized," declared CCI's Anea Bergen, beating CNN's Jan Sharp and UPN's Chet Rogers to the story by a full fifteen seconds.

Rogers, not to be outdone, was the first to detail the spectacular arrival of Ivan Tretiak.

"Not since Lenin's arrival at Finlandia Station," intoned the seasoned reporter, "has such a transformative leader made such an auspicious entrance."

Tretiak, standing victorious atop a tank turret,

greeted the cheering crowd. Every gesture and expression was amplified and exaggerated by the state-of-the-art sound system and diamond-bright video screens.

If the previous Tretiak rallies were equal to rock concerts, this one was pure theater. Tretiak may have ranted against the evils of Hollywood, but this Red Square production—complete with cast, sets, props, lighting, heroes, and villains—was as lavish as any celluloid adventure.

"Friends! Countrymen! *Russians!*"

The crowd screamed approval.

"You've no doubt heard of this morning's Senate-ordered inquiry into the shocking affairs of President Karpov," began Tretiak, "and recovered from his secret files, locked within his private safe . . ." On cue a spotlight hit the actual safe—an important visual aid adding further authenticity to Tretiak's dramatic presentation.

"The secret documents, soon to be published for all to read, prove the evil profiteer Karpov was about to squander over forty trillion of our precious Russian rubles in a crooked scheme to save his corrupt hide!"

The crowd bellowed like electric bulls, and a spotlight illuminated a second platform that looked like a gallows. On the platform, standing tall and retaining his dignity, was President Karpov.

Another roar swelled in the crowd's throat, impressed and excited by Tretiak's multimedia approach to seizing power by brazen will.

Another spotlight splashed its light on the platform, highlighting none other than Simon Templar.

"To add insult, Karpov was going to pay a king's ransom to this *international criminal!*"

Tretiak pointed dramatically at the Saint while the video screens showed the surveillance photo of Templar fleeing through the corridor of Tretiak Industries.

"Yes! There he is, running for his life after an attempted robbery right here in Moscow! International police are searching everywhere for him, but we've captured him—the notorious Simon Templar, alias the Saint—thief, terrorist, scoundrel, and a man who, this very evening, was found in President Karpov's bedroom!"

The crowd had some difficulty visualizing the scene as implied by Tretiak, but they managed to hiss, boo, and hurl verbal insults.

Watching the telecast inside the American Embassy, Emma sat mesmerized and half-crazed with fear for Simon's safety.

Templar, mindful of the theatrical element of the presentation, offered a polite and efficient stage bow to the audience. He followed that with a warm smile and friendly wave.

Tretiak almost choked.

"This criminal and your corrupt president were going to bankrupt our national treasury!" he yelled in mock astonishment. "And for what? Let me show you!"

Yet another spotlight came to life, hitting the pièce de résistance—the bedraggled array of beakers, tubes, and a lightbulb from Botvin's lab, now displayed on the back of a flatbed truck.

"Look! Look and laugh . . . laugh to keep from crying." Tretiak was laying it on with a trowel. "This sad science project was supposed to rescue Russia from a frigid, freezing death. Do you deny this, Mr. Karpov?"

Karpov threw a glance at Templar, then responded with resonant self-assurance.

"Absolutely not! I proudly admit it!"

This was not the answer Tretiak expected, and he felt a sudden unease in the pit of his stomach.

The crowd looked from Tretiak to Karpov, from Karpov to Tretiak, but no one was looking at Simon Templar. He leaned his head down to his chest and spoke into the third button of his guard uniform.

"Send the signal—do it now!"

Miles away in Tretiak's mansion, Dr. Lev Botvin sent a remote activation signal via microwave transmission. In response, the cold fusion apparatus slowly came to life, setting chemicals bubbling in their beakers.

"Sitting stupidly on that truck," continued Tretiak, regaining his authoritative demeanor, "is a fairy tale called cold fusion. You pass electrical current into the apparatus and there is supposed to be a chemical reaction. But just watch! It is supposed to heat this huge, cold, continent—but it can't even light up a measly lightbulb!"

He paused so as to not step on the audience's outburst of laughter. The laugh did not come. Instead, there was a mass murmur.

What the audience could see, and Tretiak could not, was the lightbulb beginning to glow.

The would-be dictator continued his anti-West diatribe.

"From the same, sick culture that gave us crack, unemployment, AIDS, gangster rap . . ." Tretiak was fighting to regain his rhythm, but he had already lost his audience to the astonishing image on the screen—the bulb glowing brighter, hotter. The flatbed truck began to sag, its tires melting under the intense heat of cold fusion.

The crowd surged forward as the bulb reached critical mass, the truck's windows shattered, and a magnificent white-hot column erupted into the dark night sky like a true beacon of hope.

The visuals were astonishing.

Tretiak, stunned, felt as if he were shrinking.

The crowd was amazed, amused, aghast, agog. Children were hoisted onto adult shoulders to witness this modern miracle of power and light, and several entrepreneurial members of the audience wished they had made arrangements for concession rights.

"It works! Karpov's cold fusion works!" The cry came from the crowd, repeated and rephrased again and again with mounting enthusiasm.

"The light gives off heat!"

Templar winked at Karpov.

"Miracle number one," said the Saint slyly.

Back at the American Embassy, the now-crowded room erupted in cheers. Emma wept for joy.

Three hundred thousand Muscovites stared at an exceedingly nervous Ivan Tretiak.

"All right, I grant that it *seems* to work to some extent . . . but who knows whether in the long run, the cost outweighs . . ."

No one was listening anymore. All attention reverted back to the glorious column of light, growing taller and brighter.

The crowd, caught up in a carnival mood, began to shout its allegiance to Karpov, their beloved president.

"Karpov! Karpov! Karpov!"

Then they said it again.

"Kar-pov! Kar-pov! Kar-pov!

General Sklarov, rapidly assessing his future prospects in the Russian military as decidedly dim, hastily approached his president.

"A thousand apologies, Mr. President, there was obviously a miscommunication somewhere in the chain of command. I intend to conduct a strenuous inquiry right away."

"Really? From where—prison?"

Sklarov was afraid Karpov would say something like that, and he was not tremendously surprised to find his fears were well founded. He decided it was best to ignore Karpov's comment and press on patriotically.

"We'll get that traitor, Mr. President," insisted Sklarov, and he began waving signals to his troops.

"Hey, Sklarov!" yelled Templar as he fanned the air with a friendly wave. "When do I get my epaulets back?"

From his vantage point on the scaffold, Simon could see the tanks begin to roll backward out of Red Square, the drivers hoping their anonymity would remain intact until they got back to the barracks. None of them would ever admit to being in Red Square the night the coup failed.

The amazing turn of events generated a maelstrom of chaos. The crowd, caught up in the energy of the moment, could have either torn Tretiak to shreds or ignored him completely.

Fearing the former, Tretiak slid from the tank, discarded his microphone, and was immediately shielded by Ilya and a phalanx of thugs.

"Get me the hell out of here," barked Tretiak, and made for his awaiting limo before the crowd could take action.

Ilya waved his Smith & Wesson, intimidating the

locals and aggravating the loyal military. As for the Saint, he was already off the scaffold and pushing his way through the throng.

The crowd backed off in fear at the sight of Ilya's weapon, but the military and Sklarov's Special Forces took a threatening stance. Ilya impulsively opened fire, blasting away at anyone in uniform, and three men fell dead in the street.

Panic and pandemonium. The military launched a close-range firefight with Tretiak's goons. Parents threw themselves atop their children, and the air was filled with screams and gunfire.

Flack-jacketed reporters and fearless journalists continued their live converge, detailing the action for an entranced worldwide audience.

"In an unexpected reversal of fortune, the Tretiak coup has suddenly collapsed," explained a breathless Jan Sharp. "It is not clear what role General Sklarov is playing in this media event turned violent—his Special Forces first seized the president. Now they are freeing him and turning on Tretiak!"

Back at Tretiak's mansion, Vereshagin watched Sklarov's reversal on television. He suddenly felt sick to his stomach. Everything had gone wrong. He had envisioned himself riding a rocket named Tretiak to power and influence in the New Russia. His self-aggrandizing hopes were now as shattered as the broken bottles in Red Square.

He quickly drank three glasses of vodka, smoked as many cigarettes, and began to shiver as if all the doors and windows were thrown wide to the winter cold.

He pondered fact upon fact, formed and reviewed and discarded plan after plan, until his weary brain shaped a plot with which he could find no fault.

It was, of course, a rather wild and desperate scheme, the kind a man such as Vereshagin forms after too many drinks taken in fear, but it was the only answer he could devise.

He stood as if in a stupor and scuffed his way across the mezzanine's highly polished floor. All around him was conspicuous luxury and grotesque overstatement. Above him hung the elaborate dual-tiered chandelier, suspended between twin towers as if it were a hangman suspended from a gallows.

"Gallows," whispered Vereshagin.

He pulled a black Berreta from the holster on his hip, placed the barrel against his temple, and watched the mansion slowly spin around him. He was the center of a dying universe.

His finger jerked the trigger.

The room stopped spinning.

In Red Square, Ilya and Tretiak dived into the limo. Hot lead slammed into the bulletproof windshield.

"Drive! Drive!" Ilya was yelling, his voice cracking with desperation.

The limo's tires screamed on pavement, the car careened wildly down the street, and Tretiak's foot soldiers were left stranded to fend for themselves.

Templar, disregarding the mayhem swirling around him, watched the limo's taillights disappear in the distance. There was only one place Tretiak could go—back to his mansion for the cold fusion formula.

A microphone was suddenly thrust into Templar's face, and he found himself staring into a camera lens.

"Simon Templar, alias the Saint, wanted by Scotland Yard!" It was Chet Rogers, angling for an exclusive. "Mr. Templar, what's your involvement with Karpov, Tretiak, cold fusion, and this failed coup?"

Templar's piratical visage filled television screens around the globe. One such TV set was situated in the communal living room of a large boardinghouse in the Gloucester Road area of London where three floors had been converted for that purpose. A motherly landlady provided breakfast and an occasional supper for her residents, among them being Inspector Teal of Scotland Yard.

He had not caught the earlier portions of the broadcast, but joined the coverage about the moment the camera first focused on the tanned and devilish features of Simon Templar.

Teal almost swallowed his gum, and soon his rotund nose was virtually pressed against the television screen.

Intimidated neither by Tretiak's plot nor uneven odds, Templar was even less cowed by electronic media. He felt much as he did re-entering London at Heathrow Airport, sensing that Teal himself was on the other side of the glass—which, of course, he was.

"Tretiak is a power-mad criminal attempting to kill democracy and establish a new dictatorship in Russia."

Rogers, thrilled with these sound bites, felt a rush of professional adrenaline.

"But what about you—why are you here? Are you a criminal or a hero "

Teal yelped at his television. "Criminal, dammit!"

The Saint's eyes scanned the crowd's perimeter, searching for signs of Frankie.

"If I can stop Tretiak and rescue cold fusion, let the world decide if I deserve praise or punishment."

"Simon!"

It was Frankie piloting a Zhiguli motorcycle, complete with vintage sidecar.

"Excuse me; time to play hero," said Templar to the reporter as he climbed in. "Oh. One more thing." The Saint could not resist an admirable addendum, intoned in his most authentic and unquestionably sincere British accent: "God Save the Queen!"

Across the U.K., the cheers and acclaim were, with a singular exception, unanimous. Claude Eustace Teal, had he not been so reserved, would have wept.

4

Frankie negotiated through the chaos with breathtaking confidence.

"Nice to see you again!" exclaimed Templar. "You're right, this is a classic."

"Yeah, and my timing's good, too!" yelled Frankie over the cycle's roar. "How'd you pull off that stunt in Red Square?"

"Botvin and I have been in close communication ever since I visited his lab and wired him up. It was a close call, but Karpov, Botvin, and I cooked up that little miracle before Sklarov came crashing in."

Frankie shook her helmeted head in amazement. "That was quite a miracle, even for a Saint."

"I'll need a couple more before this is over, Frankie. All hell is going to break loose at Tretiak's."

*   *   *

Simon should have used the present tense. The gates of Tretiak's estate were already flung wide open, and the staff was fleeing like proverbial rats.

Ilya and Tretiak, out of the limo and into the mansion, were racing about wildly. The younger was yelping orders at Igor and Vlad.

"Clean out the safes! Jewels, cash, passports! Hurry!"

Ilya dashed into his room, retrieved a gram vial of Methadrine, and grabbed his walking stick.

Tretiak almost stumbled over the body of Vereshagin at the foot of the winding staircase. The chief operating officer lay dead. Half his head was missing, but the weapon responsible was easily found in Vereshagin's hand.

"Suicide! You damned coward!"

Tretiak kicked the corpse before continuing up the stairs.

Frankie's motorbike-and-sidecar combination raced over the icy road to Tretiak's mansion, slush and snow spraying from the spinning tread. Above them, Simon heard the distinctive sound of helicopters—an airborne armada of news choppers en route to document the adventure's climax.

She pushed the bike full throttle, and the wind lashed them with invisible whips. The iced air stung Templar's cheeks and almost froze his lungs. Holding his two-way communicator close to his lips, he shouted a warning to Botvin.

"I'm on my way. Watch out for Tretiak!"

He had no way of knowing if Botvin could hear him or understand him over the engine's roar and the whipping wind, but he at least owed him the effort.

Botvin could hear him, but making out every word

was more than difficult. He sat at his computer, fogged glasses in his lap, downloading the cold fusion formula onto disk.

He turned when he heard the door creak.

"Mr. Templar," said Botvin to the blurry silhouette, "I make a disk for you, of full cold fusion formula."

"Templar? You said *Templar?!*"

Tretiak was enraged.

Botvin put on his glasses. A lump rose in his throat and his stomach sank.

"You traitor!" Tretiak screamed as he pulled out his gun.

"No, I'm not a traitor," insisted Botvin proudly. "I have given my talents for the future of Russia."

"You've also given your life," snarled Tretiak, and he shot Botvin point blank in the forehead. The scientist pitched backward in his chair, then slumped lifeless to the floor.

Tretiak pocketed his gun, sat down in the bloodstained chair, and swiveled toward the computer. The formula was almost finished downloading.

"I may have lost the Kremlin," said Tretiak triumphantly to Botvin's dead body, "but to control cold fusion gives me more power than the president of any country."

He ejected the priceless disk and spun the chair away from the computer. As the chair swiveled, he found himself facing Ilya. His son was pointing a gun at him.

"Gee, Dad, I was just thinking the same thing."

Tretiak laughed nervously. "What an absurd situation! My own son holding a gun on me! Don't be ridiculous, Ilya, put that away."

He did not put it away.

"A son must annihilate a father, one way or another," stated Ilya dispassionately, "if he's to be a man. . . ."

Tretiak attempted looking deeply into his son's eyes. They were not that deep. All Tretiak saw was madness fueled by Methadrine.

The universe seemed to tilt out of kilter, and the floor rumbled from approaching loyalist tanks—heavy firepower under the direction of returned turncoat General Sklarov.

As the first tank rolled up catty-corner to the mansion, Frankie's motorcycle skidded to the main gate.

The Saint leaped from the sidecar.

"Wait here, and keep the motor running."

Two gunshots rang out from inside the mansion.

Templar and Frankie exchanged looks, and he was immediately sprinting for the front door. He was almost there when Vlad and Igor, eager to escape, erupted from the entrance.

The tank gunner opened fire. Vlad and Igor died in a hail of bullets, and another salvo of shells chased Templar into the vestibule. He slammed the massive door behind him as more bullets splintered the entrance frame, but he was already well inside.

He sidestepped Vereshagin's body and ascended the stairs to the mezzanine. Resting atop an expensive antique end table was Ilya's meth vial and the deadly walking stick.

Templar crept to Botvin's office. The door ajar, he stole a silent glimpse.

Two men lay dead—Botvin and Tretiak.

Ilya was bent over his father's corpse, straining to pry the diskette from Tretiak's death grip—a grip so unrelenting that Ilya had to set down his precious gun and pull on the disk with both hands.

"C'mon Pop, give it up," growled Ilya. "Even with a bullet in the brain, you still want the world."

With a firm yank, he finally pulled the disk free.

"Sorry, Dad. You can't be a billionaire and a Communist at the same time."

"Or a rap star and Russian tsar," commented the Saint, "Fine way for a son to talk to his departed father."

Ilya's face flushed with surprise. He turned, knowing he would dread the sight of Simon Templar alive, unforgiving, and armed with Ilya's own gun.

"Hey, have pity on me," said Ilya, smiling stupidly. "I'm an orphan."

"That's the only thing we have in common," answered Templar coldly.

The arriving tanks' low frequency rumble vibrated the mansion's steel bones and timber sinews. No less taut was the tension between Ilya and Templar as Simon backed him out onto the beautifully appointed mezzanine.

The men could feel the artillery-generated vibrations increasing in intensity.

"You shouldn't be messin' with me, Templar," Ilya spat as if he were in a position to make threats. The mad Russian then stood firm as if his boots were Super-Glued to the highly polished parquet floor. He threw back his head and laughed.

"I could be runnin' this country by morning."

"You're standing on shaky ground, Sonny Boy," drawled Templar casually. He pointed the massive Smith & Wesson at Ilya's chest. "Simon says: 'Give me the disk.' "

Ilya brayed like an ass and squared his shoulders.

"You're good with those cute little Santa's Workshop sort of gadgets, but that's not one of your high-tech electronic toys, Templar, that's my goddam Smith and Wesson—a *man's* gun—no modems, no microchips. You can't handle it."

Simon understood he was in the presence of a lunatic.

Gunfire from the courtyard suddenly shattered the window, and both men dived to the floor. Glass shards shredded the velvet curtains as the bullets drilled smoking pockmarks into the wall.

When the shooting stopped, Ilya cautiously raised his eyes. Templar was aiming the weapon's gleaming steel barrel directly at his forehead.

"I can handle this better than you can handle cold fusion," insisted Templar evenly.

"They're shooting at us, for God's sake!" Ilya barked.

Templar's grip tightened on the trigger.

"Perhaps killing scoundrels has replaced freezing to death as the national pastime."

Ilya's eyes banged back and forth in their sockets as if seeking some overlooked avenue of escape.

"The disk," hissed Ilya through clenched teeth, his voice dripping with desperation. "I'll slide you the damn disk, you slide me the gun, we'll both get the hell out of here. A promise, a pact, a treaty."

He held the blue plastic nervously between his fingers, placed it on the floor, and prepared to propel it toward Templar.

"On the count of three?" He was almost begging.

Templar nodded agreement.

"One, two . . ."

The Smith & Wesson clattered across the floor as the disk did the same. Both men were on their feet in an instant.

Several more shots screamed in from outside, but Ilya ignored them. He pointed his weapon directly at the Saint.

"The disk, Templar. Give back the disk."

All things considered, Templar shouldn't have been surprised.

"But we traded," he objected, "disk for gun. A treaty, a pact, a promise."

"A Magnum outweighs promises," insisted Ilya, "especially when I'm the one holding it."

Templar shrugged and twirled the disk between his fingers. "An empty weapon makes for an equally empty threat," he noted coolly. "You said that was a six-shooter. I may not be a college graduate, but my math skills are adequate. You fired four times in Red Square, two here."

Ilya swore.

"I have cold fusion," said Templar, tucking the blue disk into his shirt pocket. "Your future is all used up."

A high-pitched wail sliced the air, and both men froze where they stood, disbelieving but decoding the sound's source: the metallic scream of incoming artillery.

The massive concussion as the first missile broad-sided the steel dome rocked the mansion into a dizzying maelstrom of falling plaster and raining crystal. Molten shards splattered onto the freshly varnished parquet, transforming it into a lake of fire. Long sheets of flame swept greedily over the draperies while smaller flames leaped with fierce eagerness up the blackening banisters of the wide spiral staircase rising from the mezzanine toward the scaffolding above.

The second blast came quickly, accompanied by additional gunfire from the courtyard. The room shuddered with heat, chaos, and confusion.

Templar ran for the stairs, grabbing Ilya's walking stick in the process. With the ground floor and mezzanine afire, there was no where to go but up. Templar took the stairs four at a time with Ilya directly behind him.

The third rocket blast rippled the staircase as if it were an amusement park ride, and the two men gripped the banisters, battling for balance.

At the top of the stairs Templar leaped to the scaffold as another shock wave shook the mansion. He stumbled, sprawled headlong, and the walking stick flew from this grip. Plaster showered down around him. Dust and debris were everywhere.

Ilya, armed and triumphant, mounted the scaffold and edged closer.

The two men locked eyes.

"Maybe I'm better at math than you," mocked Ilya. "I shot three men in Red Square, not four."

"I admit you're a master of division," offered Templar, his right hand searching under the plaster. His fingers found the tapered form of Ilya's walking stick.

"You will give me the disk and I will shoot you," stated Ilya flatly as he raised the weapon. "Or, if you prefer, I will shoot you and take the disk. Either way you are a failure and a fool."

"Fool?" Templar hoped Ilya would move even closer. His hopes were not disappointed.

"You allowed yourself to be influenced by a woman.

I, myself, have never allowed a woman to influence me."

"I bet that broke her heart," said Simon Templar, and he swung the stick with astonishing force into Ilya's right wrist. The Russian screamed in pain, and the gun spat flame as it plummeted to the inferno below.

"You were right," said Templar. "There was one bullet left."

Another missile rocked the mansion's foundation. Templar stood and steadied himself, brandishing the walking stick as if it were a sword.

Ilya's eyes widened in shocked realization—the gun was gone, Simon had the disk, flames were rapidly mounting, and missiles were blasting the mansion to rubble.

Templar thrust the stick repeatedly at Ilya, forcing him backward. "Tell me again about being a fool and a failure."

"Bastard!" yelled Ilya. "Who the hell do you think you are?"

Templar stopped. That was a good question. He hadn't know the answer for decades. But now, in this precise moment, he knew exactly who he was.

"My name is Templar, Simon Templar," he recited, saying it with the same exuberant self-assurance as he had to little Agnes those many years ago, "crusading Saint and hero of a thousand adventures."

"Spare me," groaned Ilya, and blindsided Templar with a roundhouse kick. The walking stick dropped from Templar's grip as he flailed backward over the scaffold. He clutched desperately at the struts, his strong fingers clamping like iron. He hung there, helpless, suspended over searing flames and suffocating smoke.

Ilya realized only moments remained before Templar could no longer hold on. When he fell, the cold fusion disk would be lost forever. He leaned over, quickly lifted the disk from Templar's pocket, and placed it in his own. Ilya grabbed the walking stick and began a frantic climb upward toward the domed ceiling, where a row of windows offered his only chance of escape.

He was starting to scale the scaffolding when Templar, summoning astonishing strength born of pure will, somersaulted back onto the platform.

Ilya whirled at Templar's unexpected reappearance, and what he saw unnerved him more than the renewed whine of incoming ordinance or the increased heat of rising flames.

He had left his adversary dangling above a pit of fiery death, but now Simon Templar stood before him radiating confidence and victory.

"I'm not done with you yet, Sonny Boy!" Templar shouted over the roar of flame and scream of firepower.

Ilya threw a wild look at him, and saw Templar holding aloft what appeared to be computer disk.

"I won't be suckered!" yelled Ilya. "I saw you . . ."

"The hand is quicker than the eye, my friend," said Templar proudly. "It's the first thing you learn in my line of work."

Ilya stopped cold, searching Templar's masklike face for any clue to the truth.

"That's a blank disk from Botvin's lab," stated Ilya, and he hoped he was right.

"Or is yours . . . ?"

The Russian paused only a moment to consider the possibilities. He was going out the window with *his* disk, right one or not. Reaching the top, Ilya crawled to a bracing strut that led to one of the windows. As deft as he was daft, he gingerly stepped along the plank leading to freedom.

He was halfway to his goal when incoming firepower hit the roof. The shattering explosion demolished Ilya's escape hatch and blasted him back through the air.

In a move both desperate and inventive, Ilya saved himself from plummeting into the flames by hooking the crook of his walking stick onto the lower ring of the massive chandelier suspended from the mansion's dome.

He hung there, helpless and terrified, while flames swept over the scaffold.

Templar felt the structure on which he stood ominously shift. Having only moments before the entire tower collapsed upon him, his options for action were decidedly limited.

He leaped off the crashing scaffold, clamped his grip around Ilya's ankles, and swayed over the inferno like a spider dangling from a thread.

Ilya screamed, Simon held tight, and the rope supporting the chandelier strained and stretched.

"No! Let go!" Ilya tried to kick, but his legs were locked in Simon's grip.

The wildly rocking chandelier shed a blizzard of crystal as Templar literally climbed up the screaming Russian. Templar planted his heel firmly on Ilya's head as he reached the chandelier itself.

The rope, never meant to support the additional weight of two men, began to slip. The chandelier lurched and dropped sickeningly, swaying even more precariously as Ilya shimmied up onto it, also.

The pair balanced on opposite sides, suspended over the pit of hell.

The roar of flames was loud on every side. The stifling heat drenched their brows with sweat; acrid smoke stung their nostrils and burned their lungs.

"Damn you," rasped Ilya. "Cold fusion will die with me!"

"Not exactly," insisted Templar as he again held up the disk. "I told you I had the real one, and I still do."

Infuriated, confused, and frustrated, Ilya snatched the disk from Templar's hand. It crumbled under his grip—it was nothing more than Templar's card of the Kremlin ground-plan.

In the instant of distraction Templar grabbed between Ilya's knees for the walking stick still hooked on the steel ring.

Ilya swore and his heart pounded madly in his chest.

Templar thrust the point at him, the needle-sharp tip less than an inch from the assassin's neck.

"You got it backward, Templar!" yelled Ilya. "You're the thief . . . a very good one, okay? But you don't kill people, not even people like me."

"You're the exception that proves the rule," said Templar coldly. "People like you are greatly improved by death."

With awesome dexterity, speed, and nerve, Ilya grabbed the stick's shaft and twisted it from Templar's hand.

"*I'm* the killer here!" yelled Ilya victoriously as he jabbed the point repeatedly at the Saint. "*I'm* the killer."

His triumphant grin faded when he realized what

Templar had done—in the instant Ilya regained the stick, Templar plucked the cold fusion disk from the wily Russian's breast pocket.

In Templar's left hand was the disk, in his right hand was a little penknife.

The chandelier spun dizzily and Ilya laughed hysterically. The contrast between his three-foot weapon and Simon's three-inch knife made him roar with mirth.

"And what do you plan to do with *that?*"

Templar secured the disk before offering an explanation. "You broke the law, Ilya."

"So what! You're a thief!"

Ilya punctuated his pronouncement with another easily avoided thrust.

"I don't mean that kind of law—not rules and regulations," said Templar as he climbed higher, pulling himself up the thick rope from which the opulent light fixture was suspended.

Ilya didn't understand.

"Gravity, Ilya . . . not just a good idea, it's the law."

Above the swaying chandelier, Templar reached down and sliced cleanly through the rope with his penknife's razor-sharp blade.

Ilya, riding the chandelier down into the inferno, screamed all the way to his death.

The chandelier crashed through the foyer and beyond, smashing through a second fire-engulfed wooden floor, then plummeting another forty feet into a hidden substructure below the mansion.

Ilya's death ride ended on a solid block of concrete, the chandelier shattering like a crystal bomb.

Templar swayed over the scene, momentarily awestruck by the revelation of the mansion's massive underground. He turned to climb his lifeline in a desperate bid to reach the cupola itself. A glance upward confirmed the rope's security—it was threaded through a large pully welded tightly to the ceiling and firmly attached to a winch on the far side of the dome's base.

Every muscle straining, he pulled himself up, hand over hand, higher and higher. Then he heard it—the distinctive screech of another incoming shell.

The entire mansion rocked from the impact. The winch mechanism was torn asunder, the rope blasted loose, and Templar was falling to the same fiery fate as Ilya.

The rigging angrily lashed through the pully as he plunged helplessly downward. Faster and faster he fell, the flaming parquet floor rising up to meet him.

Still clinging to the useless rope, he dropped through the gapping hole created by Ilya's death-fall. His only hope of survival was the handful of hemp clutched in his powerful grip.

The dome-top pulley rattled its bolts as the rope wildly ran through, whipping and snapping in heated fury to its massive, knotted conclusion. The oversize endpiece hit the pulley full force, wedging itself intractably between unyielding metal. The sudden tightening of the rope burned the flesh in Templar's palms and almost ripped his arms from their sockets.

A few feet from death, suspended above Ilya's broken body, Simon Templar appreciated the pain as a welcome alternative to extinction. He hung there gasping, dumbly bewildered that he should still be alive.

He dropped to safety. Slowly, in breathless wonder, he turned his gaze to the extraordinary sight before him—a vast storage space, the size of several city blocks, stacked to the rafters with aisle upon aisle of jumbo oil drums. Each drum contained hundreds of gallons of precious, hoarded heating oil.

"My, my, my," said Templar appreciatively, "tricky old Tretiak hid it all in his basement."

Templar pulled the computer disk from his pocket, regarded it in the flickering light of the fire that licked the shattered timbers above him. How much money did he hold in his hand? Ten billion dollars? Twenty? Realistically, he had contacts who would eagerly cough up tens of millions for the formula encoded upon the little magnetic wheel. Wealth beyond imagining. The prospect had, until this very moment, held him in an inescapable stranglehold. It had made him rich, for certain, but what else had it made him?

He tossed the disk up into the flames. The world's only copy of Dr. Emma Russell's cold fusion formula shriveled and melted into bubbling blue plastic.

Wealth beyond imagining . . .

If he felt a pang of remorse, it was buried under an avalanche of other, nobler feelings. In a life seemingly devised of one daring escape after another, Simon Templar felt, for the very first time, that he was truly free.

"Miracle number two," whispered the Saint.

The floor above suddenly swarmed with Russian Marines foaming out the blaze, and it wasn't long before Templar saw Frankie peering down through the crater in happy disbelief.

"Hey! Look at that! You're alive! And there's enough oil there to heat all of Moscow."

"And no one to stop you," called out Templar. "No one to stop you at all."

Frankie was immediately joined by newscasters and reporters rattling off breathtaking descriptions of the mansion's fiery destruction and its recently revealed hidden treasure.

CNN's Lloyd Swain pointed his camera through the smoking hole in the foyer floor, as did his counterpart from UPN.

CNN's signal digitally bounced via Eutelsat 2, flight 3, at 16 degrees east, transponder 41, to CNN in London, who then passed it on to CNN in Atlanta by way of Maxat's Global Skylink. When the signal arrived in Atlanta, it was inserted live into CNN International as "breaking news," and was then transmitted back across the Atlantic and retransmitted all over Europe.

The digital image of Simon Templar bounced over four satellites on its way to London's television screens.

Inspector Teal sat drop-jawed in silence, absorbing every detail of the live coverage. He turned reluctantly from the TV set when his landlady informed him that he was wanted on the telephone.

The phlegmatic detective pulled his plump posterior from the comfort of his La-Z-Boy recliner, loosed a sigh, crossed the room, and placed the receiver to his ear.

It was Sir Hamilton Dorn. "Watching the news, Teal?"

Teal mumbled an affirmation. A direct call from Dorn was highly irregular.

"Does Scotland Yard have anything solid on this Templar character, anything you could use to actually press charges?"

"In reality?"

"What else is there?"

Teal cradled the telephone against his shoulder while he unwrapped a fresh stick of spearmint gum.

"If I could lay my hands on him tomorrow, I'd have no more hope of proving he stole anything than I'd have of running the Pope in for bigamy. However, we could charge him with obstructing the police in the execution of their duty. . . ." Teal left the sentence incomplete. He preferred Dorn supply the appropriate ending.

"What's the use of busting the Saint for a milk-and-cookies rap like that?" asked Dorn rhetorically, and Inspector Teal wasn't sure exactly which tack to take.

"At best he's wanted for questioning in a dozen unsolved thefts and swindles," responded the detective. "At worst, if he arrived back in London tomorrow, I could do nothing more than meet him at Heathrow and ask him if he had a good time in Russia."

There was an ominous silence on the other end of the line, and Teal feared he was about to be remonstrated by a knighted superior.

"It's not my fault, sir," stated Teal gloomily. "We aren't in the Saint's class, and some day we shall have to admit it."

Dorn cut him short. "This matter has definite international intelligence implications, Teal. I think my office should handle it directly. I'll speak to the commissioner, and you can simply let it go."

"Yes, sir."

"It's just as well," added Dorn. "With these high-profile heroics, no jury would convict him of anything. Especially after . . ."

The two men said it in unison.

"God Save the Queen."

Teal moved his gum to the other side of his mouth.

"Yes, sir. I understand."

"Good, Teal. I appreciate your cooperation. In fact, I'd like you to come by my office tomorrow and bring detective Rabbit-Hoe—"

"That's Rabineau, sir. . . ."

". . . and we'll have a nice chat."

"Yes, sir."

Sensing Teal's weariness, Dorn made an unusually friendly offer.

"I'll even buy you a beer when you're off duty."

Teal gave it serious consideration before reciting his standard reply to offers of alcohol.

"Fat men ought not to drink, but I appreciate the gesture."

"As you wish," said Sir Hamilton Dorn.

Teal returned the telephone to its cradle and plopped himself back down in front of the television. On the screen, live from Russia, Simon Templar looked every bit the hero.

5

"AM I BORING YOU, INSPECTOR?"

It was Dr. Emma Russell who asked him the question during her debriefing in Teal's office a few days after her return from Moscow.

"Don't take it personally," explained Rabineau, leaning back in her chair. "He always looks like that."

"Has this Simon Templar made any threat to contact you in the future?" asked Teal as he unwrapped another stick of gum and folded it into his mouth.

"No. Actually, he never had a chance to say much of anything to me after I started running for the embassy."

Rabineau drummed her well-manicured fingers on the desk. She was a recent graduate of Lord Trenchard's famous Police College, and usually gave the impression of being very well satisfied with her degree.

"Quite a charmer, though, isn't he?" offered Rabineau. "The Saint, I mean."

Emma was guarded in her reply, but attempted to sound spontaneous.

"I admit he holds a certain short-term appeal. But if you're referring to romance, all I got from Mr. Templar in Moscow was a series of near-death experiences."

"Count yourself lucky," insisted Teal. "Simon Templar is our top suspect in the Uffizi bombing in Florence a few years back. . . ."

"An innocent woman was killed, along with two children," added Rabineau.

Emma took the bait, snapping out an impassioned objection.

"No! He's no murderer, Inspector. . . ."

The two detectives exchanged glances. It had been a test, and Emma failed. Belatedly she sensed it.

"Or . . . maybe he is . . . who knows?" She was unconvincing.

Teal sat close to her and did his best to appear compassionate.

"It's not unusual for kidnap victims to become enamored with their captors, Dr. Russell."

Emma's cheeks flushed.

"Simon Templar may be the Saint—and, from the looks of that Russian business, even a hero—but he's obviously also a thief, a fraud, a criminal. He stole your life's work, don't forget. He isn't a romantic hero, he has no lofty motives. Tell me, Dr. Russell, has his stolen wealth benefited anyone except himself?"

There was only one honest answer.

"No."

Teal took her hand as would a well-intentioned clergyman.

"The Simon Templar who endangered your life in Moscow is not exactly the Robin Hood of modern crime."

Emma sighed, nodded, and checked her watch. She couldn't wait to get out of there.

"Look, there's an important conference coming up. I've got to prepare my talk."

Teal walked her to the door while Rabineau pretended to do paperwork.

"We understand. The British Physicists Conference, isn't it? Been a lot of publicity about that one, several famous scientists making presentations. You have a life. We appreciate your taking the time."

Emma smiled her best professional smile and left without looking back. Teal shut the door and turned to Rabineau.

"The situation seems perfectly obvious, Inspector Rabineau," said Teal drowsily. "She's in love with him."

The hand-drawn map in the nervous grip of Dr. Emma Russell led her VW Bug down a winding English country road.

She had been perfectly honest in most of her comments to Inspector Teal—Simon Templar had not threatened to make contact with her. The fact that he had made contact indirectly and discreetly that very morning by leaving a detailed map to his whereabouts on the front seat of her car was an item best left out of official conversations.

Emma, to be fair in representing her moral and ethical dilemma, argued with herself quite intently about whether or not it was wise to rendezvous with the Saint. Returning first to Oxford, she admonished herself aloud while primping in front of a mirror.

"You're smitten like a schoolgirl, Emma," she advised herself, "and you really should have nothing further to do with him."

She laughed at her own daring absurdity, walked out to her little VW Bug, and pointed it toward Bath, Avon.

"Purified by our kisses," recited Emma, "we are healed."

She found a certain irony in the history of her destination, for Bath's fame rested on cleansing and purification.

According to a legend of which Emma was particularly fond, it was in 500 B.C. that Prince Bladud discovered the amazing curative powers of the natural hot springs. Afflicted with leprosy, he saw his swine healed of skin ailments after wallowing in the mud. He followed their example and was cured. It occurred to Emma Russell that perhaps she was only doing some mud wallowing of her own, but she preferred envisioning a more romantic and transformative outcome.

After all, she reasoned, when the Romans arrived in the first century A.D. they transformed Bath into England's first spa resort, complete with a temple, theater, and even a gymnasium.

"From mud to majesty," murmured Emma, "good things can come from unpleasant beginnings."

And she thought of Simon Templar.

There was no way around her emotions. She was fascinated, enthralled, attracted, and fearful. The fear fueled the fire of her attraction.

The Saint had deceived her, rescued her, stolen

from her, and given her freedom. He was the most astonishing combination of heroism and terrorism imaginable—a mystery more complex, elusive, and compelling than cold fusion itself.

Despite numerous opportunities to reverse direction an return to the familiar security of her tiny apartment and slowly swimming fish, Emma kept a firm foot on the gas pedal and an ongoing inner dialogue. The outcome of her internal debate was no surprise.

Emma was in love.

She followed the map's directions perfectly.

The commissioner of Scotland Yard tugged relentlessly at his thinning mustache.

"The boys from Fleet Street are having a field day with this one, Teal." He waved the *Evening Clarion* as if he could make it disappear. He couldn't.

The silver-headed superior let go of his tattered lip hairs and slammed his fist on the table.

"Front page material," continued the commissioner in his most authoritative dramatic tone, "byline by feature reporter Barney Malone, accompanied by a delightful photo of Simon Templar, alias the Saint—Scotland Yard's Most Wanted Man—performing heroics in Russia. 'Saint Saves Russian Democracy!' 'International Criminal or New World Hero?' "

He attempted throwing the newspaper against the wall, but it only flapped to the floor.

"The press loves making us look foolish, and you've made them so happy I'm surprised this Barney Malone fellow hasn't proposed marriage."

His monologue came to an abrupt conclusion, either from frustration or a lack of fresh verbiage. Teal chewed slowly, his lids hovering close to closing.

The commissioner stared at his melancholy chief inspector and shook his head in dismay.

"Do you have anything to say, Inspector Teal?"

Teal had plenty he would like to say, but his experience and professionalism forbade it.

"Sir," he began calmly, "this Saint fellow is obviously a most unpredictable character with a lot of excess energy and some rather personal ideas of justice above the law. He also seems to be exerting some degree of influence over the judgement and emotions of Dr. Russell, not to mention the president of Russia, who wants to pin a medal on him."

"Yes, I read that in the paper."

"They are enamored of one another. . . ."

"Karpov?"

"Russell and Templar," clarified Teal. "I have no doubt that she knows his whereabouts, and if he is back in the U.K. or not. I also believe that she was not forthright with us in her debriefing upon her return from Moscow."

"No doubt."

Teal chewed faster.

"Whatever is really going on with the Saint is definitely tied in to this entire Tretiak business and international espionage regarding cold fusion."

Teal paused. By broaching international espionage, he was tossing the proverbial ball onto a court out of his jurisdiction.

The commissioner leaned back in his chair and projected a thoughtful air. The detective allowed his meditating superior an appropriate measure of silence.

When the commissioner next spoke, the presentation took Teal by complete surprise.

With his mustache in one hand, he arose from his

chair, came out from behind the desk, walked over in front of Inspector Teal, and sat down on the desk's edge. He leaned forward and spoke in hushed tones.

"I'm going to ask you a question, Teal. And I want you to answer it as if your entire career depended upon the honesty of your answer, because it does."

The detective's languid lids snapped open as if they were window shades.

"I beg your pardon. . . ."

"Listen to me and answer me with absolute veracity," insisted the commissioner.

Teal stopped chewing.

"I need to know, right now, between the two of us . . ." he leaned so close to Teal that he almost fell off the desk. "Has Sir Hamilton Dorn given you any special instructions regarding Simon Templar of which I may be unaware?"

In his three decades with Scotland Yard, Chief Inspector Claude Eustace Teal had never before found himself in such a politically charged position. Had he been a man of lesser intellect, he would have blurted out the honest answer immediately. He was not a man of lesser intellect.

He eyed his superior drowsily and appeared to stifle a yawn.

"You are well aware, sir, that had Sir Hamilton Dorn instructed me to do anything, and had he invoked confidentiality necessitated by national security, I would have to comply with his request."

The commissioner slapped his thighs.

"So, do you mean to tell me that Dorn wanted the Saint to vanish in Moscow, not to be seized and extradited?"

Teal felt the balance of power shift in his favor.

"I didn't exactly say that, sir. But I think you and I can reach an understanding." If he could have forced a convincing smile, he would have.

The commissioner smiled encouragingly.

"If you would be so kind as to take me into your confidence regarding the matter, I'll do the same," offered Inspector Teal.

Fair enough.

The commissioner stood and began pacing about the office.

"Politics, Teal. Damn politics. You know how I hate it when we get the rug pulled out from under us by Special Branch or MI5. . . ."

Teal mumbled and nodded.

"I know British Intelligence is having fits about Tretiak, Templar, Russia, and this whole Russell affair. They have no reason to tell us anything more than they want to. And that means this so-called Saint could be a clandestine operative of Her Majesty's government, the CIA, or even the French. The French!"

The commissioner had a personal problem with the French.

"If Simon Templar is a deep-cover agent, or if he's been drafted or pressured into serving some major player in the intelligence community, Sir Hamilton Dorn would be perfectly happy to let Scotland Yard look foolish and incompetent if it served what he calls 'the greater good.'"

"I'm sure it's happened before, sir," agreed Teal.

"Damn right! Not that I don't support the best interests of the Crown, mind you, but if Dorn's messing with a priority investigation of Scotland Yard and not informing me of it . . ."

Teal looked more tired than ever.

"And so," added the dour detective, "there is the possibility that certain government agencies have a vested interest in keeping Simon Templar out of jail and up to his neck in international intrigue. He could be on his own, or under someone's thumb."

The commissioner stood at the window combing the remains of his mustache.

Teal stood and held his bowler over his protruding stomach.

"Well, Teal, tell me."

"The honest answer is that Simon Templar, despite the massive media attention given his antics in Russia, managed to disappear from Moscow. He has not, to this point in time, been apprehended. That does not mean that if we bring him in, that Sir Hamilton Dorn wouldn't arrange his release for purposes of, shall we say, 'voluntary conscription.'"

Perfect.

Teal managed to confirm his failure while deflecting attention and suspicion back on Sir Hamilton Dorn.

"Of course," added the detective, "were Dorn to arrange a release on the condition that Templar serve Her Majesty's government, it would be in the national interest."

"Oh, yes. Absolutely."

"And in such a situation, I'm sure that you would be the first informed, and perhaps the only one so informed. After all, I may be chief inspector, but you're the commissioner of Scotland Yard."

The tiny comb returned to the commissioner's pocket. He turned and smiled warmly at Inspector Teal.

"Thank **you. Thank you** for your honesty and dedication, Inspector."

Teal nodded.

"Do you have any idea where this Templar may have gone, or what he may do?"

The detective's bowler hat began moving in circular motions, propelled by pudgy fingers.

"We haven't seen the last of him. He's out there, somewhere. Wherever he is, whatever the reality of the situation, there's one thing we know for sure—Dr. Emma Russell is in love with him. That means the feeling may be mutual. If so, there is an off chance that Templar will show up at the physicists convention at Oxford tomorrow."

The commissioner cocked his head.

"Were you and Rabineau planning to be there?"

Teal shifted his ample weight.

"As I said, it's an off chance. There is tremendous security for the event as it is, sir."

"Be there, Teal. Even if it is a waste of time, we need to have a strong presence. Dorn's men will be, probably disguised as *gentlemen.*"

It was clear that the masculine descriptive was not intended as a compliment.

Between Oxford and Bath, half hidden in the deep woods, was a secluded farmhouse which, despite the corporate shell who's name adorned the deed, was among the property assets of Simon Templar.

This isolated abode was one of the Saint's more rustic temporary residences. He owned or leased several habitats. in numerous residential areas under a variety of names.

There was an impressive apartment maintained at #7 Upper Berkely Mews in the name of Sebastian Tombs, another at Cornwall House in Piccadilly leased to Louis Hayward, and a rather respectable-looking house in Home Counties Weybridge sold to a wealthy gent calling himself Hugh Sinclair. All these men were the Saint, and all these properties were utilized for his diverse purposes.

Today the purpose was romance.

Dr. Emma Russell turned off her car's ignition and waited for the VW's engine to rattle its way to silence before setting the hand brake. She eagerly pulled the Bug's reluctant and wobbly handle and gave the door an encouraging shove with her shoulder. She exited, took a deep breath, and walked toward the farm-house door.

It was unlocked. She let herself in.

Feeling a bit like Goldilocks sneaking into the Three Bears' cottage, Emma looked around the rustic rooms. There was no porridge on the stove, but there was a warm fire glowing from the bedroom hearth.

On the nightstand next to the bed were her seven cold fusion cards. Standing next to them was Simon Templar, alias the Saint.

"You can take your cards and go if you want."

For a moment she couldn't speak. She had last seen him at the American embassy, disguised as Straubing. Today he stood before her as no one but himself, his eyes gleaming with mocking humor and honest romance.

"I'm not going anywhere," said Emma. The entire room seemed to glow from the fire in her heart.

He swept her into his arms, and they kissed as if it were a grand swashbuckling adventure. For them, it was.

"My hero!" exclaimed Emma, and they both laughed as they tumbled onto the bed.

They kissed several more times before Simon spoke to her in the lisping voice from the first day they met.

"I'll expoth her for the fraud thee ith!"

Emma gasped and giggled. "That was you?"

"Yeth. I mean, yes. That's who I thought Dr. Russell would like," admitted Templar with self-deprecating humor. "I thought she was going to be some old biddy."

"I will be an old biddy someday, and you'll be right after all." Emma patted his shoulder encouragingly.

"I didn't know Dr. Russell was a gorgeous soon-to-be-trillionaire," continued Templar. "You're going to be the richest woman in the world."

"I am?"

Templar pulled her close.

"Sure. Why do you think I'm hanging around?"

He kissed her and she kissed him back. They replicated this interpersonal chemistry experiment several times in rapid succession before Templar leaned back and stared at the ceiling.

"Emma, my life is very strange. I told you about when I was a kid, the orphanage. . . ."

She kissed his cheek and put an arm around him.

"I got out of there when I was thirteen, ran away, and lived on the street. I made it all the way to America on stealth, wits, and stealing. I thought I was winning, but all I was doing was amassing numbers in a bank balance."

Emma held him closer. "Did you hurt a lot of people, Simon?"

"I robbed a lot of people. Stole money, diamonds, art, time, emotion, trust. And *I* was *good* at it. I *am* good at it. But. . . ." His voice trailed off.

"Why, Simon Templar," chided Dr. Emma Russell, "I believe you're having an attack of ethics."

He smiled. He hadn't felt this open, this free, since his childhood.

"There's an expression I heard once that I paid no attention to," acknowledged Templar. "It went like this: Your resentments will kill you. I was about the most resentful guy on the planet—almost fifty million dollars in the bank and I only felt alive when I was stealing something, trying to get back what was stolen from me—and that, of course, is . . . stupid . . . insane . . . nutsy-coo-coo."

He suddenly rolled over on top of her and kissed her firmly and loudly on the nose.

"Hey, Mr. Wet Kisser!" She laughed, but couldn't help arching beneath him as if they were lovers.

"My name is not Mr. Wet Kisser," he insisted playfully. "The name is Templar, Simon Templar—the hero of a thousand adventures."

"How's this for an adventure, Mr. Templar?"

She kissed him with compelling passion.

At length, when they came up for air, he offered his commentary.

"A thousand adventures like that and I'll be the world's weakest swashbuckler."

She propped herself up on her elbows. "Unbuckle your swash," she intoned wickedly, "the adventure has yet to begin."

"Why Dr. Ruthell," lisped a compliant Templar seductively, "You thertainly are ecthiting."

"Yeth," she agreed.

"Sounds to me like there's something wrong with your tongue."

She convinced him otherwise, and they savored the evening together.

During a pause from their more animated moments of interaction, Templar rested his head against her chest. He heard the sound of her heart, listened to her breathing, and touched her gently.

"I wonder if George Sanders started like this," murmured the Saint.

Emma chuckled. "Very suave, that Mr. Sanders," agreed Emma. "He was married to both Zsa Zsa Gabor and her sister."

"Not at the same time, of course."

"Certainly not," Emma said it with a dollop of high-society intonation.

"Sanders and I have a lot in common," remarked Templar cryptically.

"Were you also married to Zsa Zsa? If so, I want all the details," purred Emma in her best Gaborian accent. "After all, Zsa Zsa is considered the embodiment of all things good in bed."

"I'd like to see her prove that in a court of law," said Templar, and they both paused to visualize the presentation of evidence before he continued. "George Sanders and I both have fake names, we were both ripped off by Russian gangsters, and we both got out of Russia in the nick of time—my departure being more recent than his, of course."

"You pulling my leg?"

"My pleasure, darling. But no, this is ironic fact. He was born in St. Petersburg. His father was the bastard son of Prince von Oldenburg and one of the czar's sisters. The day George left Russia for school in England was the same day Lenin entered. They actually saw each other at the Finlandia train station when

Stalin, Trotsky, and the rest of those Russian gangsters came to meet him."

"Stalin came to meet George Sanders?" Emma was teasing.

Templar sighed in feigned exasperation.

"Lenin eventually confiscated all of George's family's money and killed most of his relatives. George never got over it, but he went on to become suave, debonair, famous, and then . . ."

Emma knew, and her heart skipped a beat.

"His resentments killed him," Templar said. "He committed suicide."

"And?" Emma prompted him to continue.

"And that's where the resemblance ends," said Templar as he pulled her over on top of him, "because I'm done with Russian gangsters, fresh out of resentments, finished with revenge, and madly in love with the brilliant Dr. Emma Russell."

They kissed several more times with unabated gusto.

Later, prior to drifting off to sleep in each other's arms, they spoke softly.

"How did you know all that stuff about George Sanders?"

"If I find something, or someone, of interest, I find out everything I can. I have an insatiable mind."

"So that's what you call it," remarked Emma pleasantly.

He smiled in the darkness.

"I do love to read," said Templar. "And I noticed the eclectic collection of books in your apartment. What was that one . . . ? 'The best beloved of all things in my sight is justice.' "

"Ah. *The Hidden Words of Baha'u'llah.* One of my favorites."

"That was the only one I read—I was busy casing the joint, as I recall."

"There is one quote in there that reminds me of you, Mr. Templar. I know this one by heart . . . almost, maybe." Emma cleared her throat before recitation.

" 'Thou art even as a finely tempered sword concealed in the darkness of its sheath and its value hidden from the artificer's knowledge.' " Her voice was soothing, melodic. " 'Wherefore come forth from the sheath of self and desire that thy worth may be made resplendent and manifest unto all the world.' "

"If I manifest myself too much, Teal will resplendently arrest me and drag me to a police station in Pimlico, or worse yet, Westminster—members of Parliament get taken there."

He may have been joking, but there was something about his intonation that made Emma uneasy. She nestled closer.

"After your Russian heroics, do you really worry about getting arrested?"

Templar was silent for a moment before responding.

"There's something you must understand," he said seriously. "They'll never stop hunting me. Never. On every continent there are cops who won't quit till I'm caught. I can never stop running."

Emma immediately understood what he was trying to say, and she would not have it.

"I can run, too!" She was ardent, almost pleading. "You saw me run in Moscow. I ran and I ran and my heart didn't fail. . . ."

Templar took the precious woman in his arms, and felt her tremble against him.

"Your work counts for too much, Emma. If I didn't love you, I'd let you come with me."

She fought back tears, clinging to him as if her life depended on it.

"Then what're we doing here? Everything was so wonderful, finally. You and I, like this . . . I thought . . ." Her warm tears were wet on Templar's shoulder.

"Why did you ask me to meet you here, for a one-night stand? To break my heart?" She knew the answer was neither.

He stroked her cheek tenderly, lovingly.

"So I could return what I took from you . . . and to hear you tell me that you loved me too, no matter what."

Emma held him tightly.

"I do love you," said Emma, and it was as much an entreaty at it was a confession. "I love you, I love you."

". . . *Simon* . . ."

"I love you, *Simon*."

"Miracle number three," sighed the Saint.

6

TEMPLAR AWOKE TO FIND HIMSELF ALONE. NEXT TO him, resting on Emma's pillow, were two significant items—a small stickpin of a human ideogram sporting a rakish halo, and a handwritten note of explanation and farewell.

Simon,
   The pin is something silly I've kept for years, a graduation gift from Catholic school. As you can tell from the halo, it's a saint. Don't worry, you don't have to wear it. I just wanted you to have something of mine, something I loved.

He held the pin as if it were more precious than rubies. He blinked away the emotion stinging the corners of his eyes and kept reading.

In finding the strength to go on without you, I found the courage to give away cold fusion. This morning, at the British Physicists Society Conference at Oxford, I'm giving it away to the world. My topic was to be "The Future of Cold Fusion: Promise and Possibilities," but instead I will give them the future now. It belongs to the world, Simon, not to me, not to us. We have no right to sell it. Because we don't own it, we will be free, you and I. Perhaps you don't believe that right now, but you will. Maybe some day we'll have a kinder, warmer world. A world where they'll see the light, and stop hunting you. I love you, Simon.

Forever,
Emma.

He hurriedly dressed, prepared himself for any eventuality, and blasted his Volvo toward Oxford.

The conference was as well attended as it was well publicized. Physicists and scholars representing science's diverse disciplines arrived from throughout Europe, America, Australia, Asia, and the South Pacific. Dignitaries in attendance included prominent political figures more adept at public relations than physics, and the requisite representatives of the Royal Family. The latter necessitated the prominent presence of uniformed bobbies and plainclothes agents from Special Branch.

The carefully crafted program was, as is the case with most professional conferences, structured for maximum appeal to specific passions and universal interests.

Dr. Emma Russell held no illusions concerning the

reason for her inclusion among the conference's featured presenters—she was the scientific community's mascot dreamer and semirespected iconoclast.

While her credentials were impeccable, her obsession with cold fusion was controversial. The placement of Dr. Russell in the morning session assured a stimulating jump-start to the proceedings, especially in light of the recent Russian adventure.

Emma knew she was scheduled primarily for entertainment value, controversy, and speculative newspaper copy. She not only knew it and fully accepted it, but on her drive from Templar's retreat to Oxford, she delighted in it. If revenge was sweet, vindication was sweeter—especially when it ushered in a glorious new age of unlimited heat, light, and energy.

Traffic was predictably heavy in Oxford, the "city of dreaming spires," where too many bells were always ringing in the rain. The bells of Oxford pealed out their resonant welcome through the predictably wet weather as Emma's VW putt-putted into her pre-assigned parking place.

Emma locked the car, paused to inhale an invigorating breath of crisp Oxford air, then walked with light steps to her Chemistry Building office.

On the way, she smiled at distinguished visitors admiring the campus. She read name tags and participant badges of passers-by and fellow scientists who would, in less than an hour, be astonished recipients of her love-inspired breakthrough.

Teal and Rabineau, hardy representatives of the United Kingdom's law enforcement elite, were on campus as well, hovering near a chaos of umbrellas raised against a British cloudburst.

"Do you think he might show?" asked Rabineau.

She was intently studying photographs of an unmasked Simon Templar culled from CNN's video coverage in Red Square.

Teal masticated slowly, raindrops dripping from his hat.

"How would we know if he did? With the Saint being a master of disguise," said the detective, pointing discreetly toward an enormous, dignified Samoan, "he could be that gentleman right there."

For a moment, Inspector Rabineau considered the possibility.

"If she loves him, he might love her, too. Then again, if she loves him, she sure as hell isn't going to press charges."

"She doesn't have to," Teal sighed. "If we nab him we're to bring him in for questioning—debriefing is more like it—it's Dorn and British Intelligence that want him. It's a matter of priorities—they get first crack at him, even before Interpol. Even if they can't pin anything on him, the threat of it can hang over him forever. They apparently view him as 'potentially useful.'"

Rabineau's eyes brightened. "Am I supposed to know that, Inspector?" she asked playfully.

The chief inspector pulled his collar up against the rain. "Forget I said anything," he instructed, and they both knew he didn't mean it.

A few minutes later they saw Dr. Emma Russell approaching the Shelton Theatre on foot from the Chemistry Building, bareheaded and blissfully unaware of the weather. The two detectives blended into the background and kept an eye out for signs of the Saint.

The umbrella-laden crowd was queued up outside

the theater, moving slowly through the doorways into the auditorium. Emma, in an attempt to bypass a particularly slow-moving contingent from Baycombe, moved to the crowd's edge.

She skirted the dawdlers on her right and was passing an alley between two quadrangles on her left when a balding man with thick glasses intruded on her personal space and broke her concentration.

"Excuse me, but is this where Dr. Russell is going to speak?"

"Yes, I . . . uh . . . I mean, she . . ." Momentarily flustered, Emma paused to compose herself. As she faced him, a brief bit of sunlight glinted off the stickpin in his lapel—a jaunty stick figure sporting an absurd elliptical halo.

"Oh my God. . . ." Her eyes flicked nervous reference to the abundance of law enforcement personnel on site. They flowed along with the crowd, moving toward the edge, and ducked into the alley.

"Emma," Templar spoke in his own voice, "I came to say that if you think I'm just going to sit there and watch you give away an unimaginable fortune . . ."

She held her breath.

". . . you're absolutely right."

Emma smiled. There was nothing more to say. She glanced from his disguised face to her wristwatch, and then to the theater door. It was time. As she threw him a fraught farewell look, he whispered a parting promise.

"You found me, Emma. . . . I'll find you."

She slipped back into the crowd, and joined her fellow attendees. Entering the Shelton Theatre she was soon surrounded by colleagues, press, and Oxford security.

Teal and Rabineau, still standing outside in the rain, were feeling both increasingly wet and foolish.

Teal motioned toward the theater.

"We might as well go on in."

With the auditorium filled and the perfunctory introductions concluded, the conference chairman introduced the first speaker.

". . . Dr. E. J. Russell, whose presentation is entitled 'The Future of Cold Fusion: Promise and Possibilities.' "

Emma waved away the applause as she approached the stage and prepared to take the podium.

Inspector Teal secured a seat just off the aisle near the side exit, and scanned the crowd for anyone resembling Simon Templar. His intense concentration was broken by the nasal lisp of the balding nerd who plopped himself down in the seat beside him.

"You don't thwallow thith cold futhion nonthenth, do you?"

The detective frowned at the intrusion, then resumed scrutinizing the attendees as Dr. Russell began her address.

"We know cold fusion had a difficult childhood. Those few of us in the field are orphans, bastards at best . . ."

She knew Templar was somewhere in the crowd, and her gaze soon found his bald head and thick glasses. The sight of him sitting next to Inspector Teal almost made her drop her notes.

She paused, composed herself as if searching for just the right phrase, and continued.

"But difficult childhoods, I believe," said Emma, looking directly at the Saint, "create the most interesting adults."

As not to be obvious, she turned her attention to another section of the theater.

"And today, I'm here to tell you that although practical application of cold fusion is still speculative, still years away . . ."

She turned back toward Templar, and the Saint was gone. Her voice involuntarily caught in her throat, and Teal noticed she was looking directly at him—almost.

The detective turned to the empty aisle seat beside him, then back to Emma on stage. A slight flush of pink appeared on his portly cheeks as he processed the unavoidable implication.

"Recent events in Russia," continued Dr. Russell, "have dramatically demonstrated that, in a theoretical sense at least, cold fusion has finally come of age."

Teal slowly unwrapped a fresh stick of spearmint gum, and muttered softly under his breath.

"Hell, let Dorn find the Saint himself."

Outside the theater, Simon Templar strolled undeterred toward his awaiting Volvo C70. Passing through the parking lot, he discreetly discarded the baldcap wig and geeky glasses, both of which went sailing into the nearest trash can.

He turned the ignition key and piloted the C70 out into traffic.

The businessman whose Canadian passport identified him as James Westlake of Windsor, Ontario, drove his Volvo to Heathrow in full compliance with the rules of the road. He couldn't risk a traffic ticket, and drummed his fingers on the steering wheel while listening to the BBC. The reporter detailed the current status of the restablized democratic regime in Russia, and confirmed that the notorious Simon Templar, alias the Saint, was, despite his recent heroics, still wanted for questioning in numerous international cases of high-tech theft.

Someday, Templar fancied, he would take Teal to tea and explain to him the entire sordid story. Someday. Not today, not with half of Scotland Yard and British Intelligence searching for him with arrest warrants, not with Interpol awaiting him in any country which had ever signed an extradition agreement with the United Kingdom.

"In other news," continued the BBC reporter, "a nonprofit research foundation has been established to develop cold fusion technology. Funded by an anonymous donation of fifty million dollars, the foundation is chartered to develop 'inexpensive, clean energy for the benefit of all mankind. . . .' "

EPILOGUE

Hong Kong

THE ST. IGNATIUS HOME FOR BOYS WAS NEITHER AS large nor as foreboding as Simon Templar remembered it from his childhood.

Viewed from an adult perspective, the rooms were small, the desks were tiny, and the hallways narrow.

He arrived without appointment one sunny spring day and simply asked to see the headmaster. The nun who greeted him was warm and personable. She bade him be seated.

Memories flooded his senses, bringing to the fore every emotion associated with his years at St. Ignatius.

He looked out the window and saw something he did not expect—children playing happily on an elaborate outdoor swing-set. He heard laughter and giggles, shouts of glee and delight. A smile began to light his eyes and spread to the corners of his mouth.

"The Father will see you now."

Simon smiled pleasantly at the friendly Sister and stepped inside the headmaster's office.

It was not Father Brennan whose face he saw, but the big bearded visage of a joyous, barrel-chested priest with a bearlike build.

His handshake was firm and his demeanor gregarious.

"Welcome, welcome to St. Ignatius," he began. "I'm the headmaster. What can I do for you?"

"I'm . . . I'm a graduate, or former student, or former . . ."

"Inmate?"

The blunt but accurate noun came as a surprise.

"Well, yes, honestly . . ."

"What's your name, son?"

Simon Templar looked the priest square in the eye and played a hunch.

"My name is *not* John Rossi. Never has been, never will be."

A thunderclap of recognition flashed across the priest's face. "Simon! Simon Templar!"

The Saint was swept up in the manly hug of a lifetime.

"Don't you see who's behind this fuzzy beard? It's me, Bartolo!"

"I thought so, but I wasn't sure—the beard!"

" 'Tis I, indeed, my Saintly crusader—hey, still breaking and entering?"

"Old habits . . . no pun intended," said Templar, and he recalled their friendship from years gone by.

The man who was Bartolo gave Templar the complete tour of the new and improved facility, ending at a small garden in the courtyard—a garden named in memory of Agnes.

"I never expected this," admitted Templar.

"Nothing stays the same forever, and neither do people. We all form our lives and build our futures on the experiences of the past. Take us, for example: You ran away and became a thief. I stayed and became a priest."

"I saw a movie like that once," joked Simon Templar. "You were Pat O'Brian and I was James Cagney."

"Pat O'Brian, indeed." Bartolo laughed. "You're too debonair for Cagney."

Templar looked at his old friend with heartfelt admiration. It was as if the years between them melted away. He could have sworn it was just last night that they raided the pantry.

"Brennan?" said Templar, and he needn't have said more.

Father Bartolo shrugged and cocked his head. "If I told you"—he smiled coyly—"you wouldn't believe it."

"Now you *must* tell me," insisted Templar.

Bartolo began walking around the garden. "One day, not long after you . . . you left, he became enraged about something . . . or nothing . . . it doesn't matter."

He stopped.

"The dogs turned on him. They almost ripped him to shreds. It was horrible."

"Dead?"

"No. And I'm sure he'd like to see you."

There was a sudden sinking feeling in Templar's stomach. "Like to see me?"

Bartolo motioned toward a simple bench at the

edge of the garden and checked his watch. "Let's sit. He'll be along shortly."

The two childhood pals sat down in the sun. Laughter of boys and girls at play echoed off the high stone walls. In a few minutes a tiny man came shuffling toward the garden carrying a pink plastic watering can.

"Is that him?"

A nod.

Templar stood.

He walked toward the garden, coming to a stop beside Father Brennan.

How small he seemed, barely reaching the mid-most part of Simon's chest.

The old man's eyes crinkled above the long-healed scars of what must have been a most vicious and ferocious attack. He poured water on the budding flowers and smiled up at Simon Templar. "Hello."

"Hello."

Simon stared at Brennan. Gone was the evil tyrant. Here was only an aged, infirm gardener.

"You're Father Brennan, aren't you?"

He stopped watering, and a gracious smile illumined his hard-bitten features.

"Yes, yes, I am. Do I know you?"

"Yes. I was a student of yours, years ago. I'm afraid we gave each other some rather unpleasant memories."

Templar's gaze turned involuntarily to the garden. He still wanted to punch Brennan in the nose.

Brennan searched Simon's face. "Your name?"

What the hell.

"My name is Templar, Simon Templar . . ."

The pink plastic watering can dropped from Brennan's hand. And then, to Simon's eternal surprise, Father Brennan wrapped his arms around him, rested his head on his chest, and cried.

After a moment the wet-eyed priest lifted his head and apologized.

"I've prayed for you . . . and for her, every night. . . ."

He could say no more; Templar could hear no more.

In time he rejoined Bartolo on the bench.

"Whew," Templar exhaled. "That was different than I expected." He gave Bartolo a mischievous grin.

"I couldn't exactly punch him in the nose, even though the thought crossed my mind. He's old, frail, small, and it just wouldn't be right."

Father Bartolo slapped him on the back.

"C'mon, I have something for you before you go."

It was back inside St. Ignatius that the big-bearded priest began digging through an odd collection of artifacts and literature.

"I know it's here, because I keep coming across it when I'm not looking for it," mumbled Bartolo, "and I can't imagine why Brennan didn't toss it out. Or, for that matter, why I didn't. Maybe it was . . . ahh, here it is—a little memento of our reunion."

Knight Templar.

"It's missing a few pages—the spine broke when he threw it, remember?"

"Almost beaned you, if I recall." Templar laughed, and he held the tattered paperback as if it were an authentic religious relic. "I can keep this?"

"Sure," said Bartolo. "With that buxom beauty on the cover, I think it's much better that you have it. After all, it is yours, isn't it? Or did you steal that, too?"

Simon looked down, mock-penitent. "No, I must confess that I *didn't* steal it."

He looked back up. "Thanks . . . do I call you 'Father'?"

"Brother to you, Simon."

"The Saint has a brother who's a priest—makes sense to me."

They both laughed.

Bartolo walked Templar out.

"When you're back in London, and if you're looking to do a good deed . . ."

"Good deeds are my stock and trade," confirmed the Saint.

". . . I have a friend who runs the Arbour Youth Centre on Shandy Street in Stepney. You know, providing entertainment and activities to keep kids from becoming . . . well . . ."

"Like me?"

"No, like Tretiak and Ilya."

Templar was caught up short. "You know about that?"

Bartolo laughed.

"We get CNN, UPN, ITN, CCI—there's a satellite dish on the roof."

"Modern technology at its most compassionate," affirmed the Saint.

Bartolo looked silently at Templar for a moment. "What now, my friend? From what I can tell from the news, not everyone is willing to leave you alone about your 'alleged' past. Where do you go, what do you do?"

"Well, I've been thinking about my prospects," began Templar cheerfully, "and I've discerned that

I'm a pirate or philanthropist as the occasion demands."

"Go on," encouraged Bartolo.

"When you and I were first at St. Ignatius, we were told that some day we would lose our youthful impetuosity and impatience, and settle down to a normal life."

"Yes, that's usually the pattern," agreed his friend.

"Not for me," insisted Templar happily. "This rubbing off of corners, this settling down, this normal life . . . can you picture me with the snug office, the regular hours, the respectable weekends?"

Bartolo couldn't picture that at all.

"Are you going to stay on the right side of the law?"

The Saint laughed. "When laws are outlawed, only outlaws will have laws," he quipped. "In fact, a certain Sir Hamilton Dorn of British Intelligence actually had the nerve to track me down via the Internet and offer me a job." The Saint intoned the word *job* as if it were an irritating rash or dysenteric symptom of dyspepsia.

"Well, did you at least consider it?"

"Yes," responded Templar. "I considered it foolish."

Bartolo shook his head in amusement. His childhood chum was as irreverent and impudent as ever.

"I've formulated the idea of making my life's work to register myself in the popular eye as something akin to a public institution."

"Meaning?"

"You read the paper, you watch the news—there are millions of people out there who don't have lives any better than mine was when I was a kid. Five-year-olds working in sweat shops to make soccer balls, young girls sewing fourteen-hour shifts for less than forty cents a day, and the list goes on. I figure they have things rough enough without crackpots, dictators, and other crooks robbing them blind or making it worse."

"So, you going to save the world?"

"You're not the first person to ask me that," said the Saint, and he thought of Frankie.

"The answer?"

"Well, actually, after I return to London and take a certain Scotland Yard detective to tea, I'm going to Las Vegas."

"To gamble?"

"Never. Gamblers die broke. There's a right-wing fascist arms manufacturer I read about in the paper who can't resist easy money. I plan on meeting him there and relieving him of several million dollars. A man such as I can do a lot of good with that kind of loot."

"An interesting career choice," noted Bartolo. "You'll be the Robin Hood of modern crime."

"Catchy phrase," agreed the Saint, "and while I'm at it, I might just punch *him* in the nose."

They shook hands, smiled, and then Father Bartolo watched Simon Templar walk away in the sunlight.

Halfway down the block, merging into the bustling Hong Kong crowd, Templar turned to wave again.

That was how Bartolo would always remember him—tall and smiling and debonair, one closed hand resting on his hip, his other raised in farewell.

Bartolo turned back toward the courtyard. Several energetic youngsters skipped along beside him.

"Who ya wavin' at, Father?"

"The Twenty-First Century's Brightest Buccaneer," he answered dramatically, "the most astonishing combination of heroism and terrorism ever to leap from the pages of ace pulp fiction!"

The children laughed.

They thought he was kidding.